"Get in the car. Wait," Laurent added.

He grabbed Eden and kissed her before she knew what was happening. His mouth was hard on hers, and his tongue demanding. She felt like a match being struck. All she could do was tilt her head back against his arm and ride the sudden blaze.

It was over in a moment.

He stepped back and said "Shall I drive?" as cool and calm as you please.

Eden had to lean against the car, too full of heat and confusion to think for a few moments. She finally managed to lift her head and angrily demand, "What was that about?"

He was totally insouciant, totally unashamed. "That's one of the old rules, isn't it? The hero gets to kiss the girl he just saved."

Eden made a dramatic gesture of wiping the back of her hand across her mouth. "You didn't save me."

"I saved your car."

"Then kiss the car."

She slid past him and had the car started and in gear by the time he got into the passenger's seat. "Fasten your seat belt." She hated that desire seethed in her as much as anger, and her voice sounded rough with emotion. "Where to?"

"Somewhere dark."

Master of Darkness

Also by Susan Sizemore

Crave the Night
I Thirst for You
I Burn for You
I Hunger for You
The Shadows of Christmas Past
(with Christine Feehan)

Master of Darkness

SUSAN SIZEMORE

POCKET **STAR** BOOKS

NEW YORK   LONDON   TORONTO   SYDNEY

An *Original* Publication of POCKET BOOKS

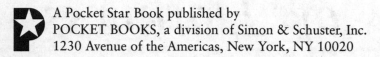 A Pocket Star Book published by
POCKET BOOKS, a division of Simon & Schuster, Inc.
1230 Avenue of the Americas, New York, NY 10020

ISBN:0-7394-6321-7

POCKET STAR BOOKS and colophon are registered trademarks of Simon & Schuster, Inc.

Cover art by Franco Accornero

Manufactured in the United States of America

For Christina Ham,
who is very dear to me

Master
of Darkness

Chapter One

The treasure was safe—Laurent wished he could say the same for himself. He was walking down a dark, deserted street, the time was approaching midnight, and frankly, he was lost.

Heading for San Diego had seemed like a good idea when he'd hightailed it out of Colorado with the stolen laptop. But this was not the San Diego he remembered from several decades before. When had he last hung out here? Sometime in the 1940s, maybe? The thirties? The place had certainly grown since then. They'd even built an aerospace museum on the site of the Ford Motor Building he used to frequent during the daytime. It just hadn't occurred to him that what had been a nice, quiet old city would change and grow with the times.

That was one of the problems with being long-lived: sometimes change came up and slapped you on the head when you thought you had a handle on it.

But his sense of displacement wasn't his major problem at the moment; staying alive was.

Justinian, the pack leader of Tribe Manticore, had already put a bounty on his head—and to think that a week ago, Laurent had been certain the old boy didn't even know how to use a telephone.

Of course, there was that telepathy thing. . . .

It wasn't that he had forgotten about their mental powers. It was just that he'd lived in Los Angeles for a long time, where the safest way for a renegade Tribe Prime to survive in the Clan-dominated territory was to stay under the psychic radar.

I should have stayed renegade. It wasn't a bad life. But no, I had to try to make peace with Justinian, with my past. Okay, I was mostly in it for the money, but—

Laurent stopped. He didn't see anyone, but the street no longer felt deserted. Instinct told him that he wasn't alone.

Not again.

Back in the day, San Diego hadn't exactly been a thriving hotbed of vampirism. But ever since he'd blown into town three nights ago, the locals had been all over him. They'd all been Tribe boys, which was why he figured Justinian was involved. If there were noble, snooty Clan types in the area, they were holed up in expensive suburbs like La Jolla just like in the old days, leaving the seedier sides of the city for his kind.

There were at least two stalking him. He couldn't hear their breathing, but when he closed his eyes and concentrated, he picked up the very faint sound of slow heartbeats. Their psychic signatures were masked, but he did pick up a trace of human energy that was not the usual background noise. Was he being tracked by humans, too?

That didn't make any sense, so he'd worry about it later. Right now he had a couple of Tribe Primes to deal with.

"Okay, nobody asked me to do this, but a little documentation might help the cause. I'm going to consider this a blog and rattle off impressions along with facts as I go along."

Eden Faveau paused to take a deep breath before she spoke into the tiny voice-activated tape recorder again. She wanted to yell, but she had enough self-possession to whisper.

"I do not want to be here, or doing this,

thank you very much, Dad, and all the other members of the only official vampire-hunting family left in the world." She took another deep breath. "Okay, that's off my chest. Actually, I could be in Hawaii right now, instead of up on a roof waiting for some vampire to show up at the *appointed place and time* as the oh-so-cryptic message from this Clan woman—local matri, I suppose—so portentously stated. I had my first two-week vacation planned—ever. And what happens? I get called upon to 'take up the mantle of responsibility for the family avocation' and fight evil because Dad and the boys have to be at some security conference in D.C."

Fight evil. Trip to Hawaii. Eden supposed that fighting evil had to be the first choice, but she had this desire to see flowing lava again. Visiting one of the Hawaiian volcanoes seemed like the safest way to do it.

"But we vampire hunters don't do things the safe way, now do we?" she spoke sarcastically to the recorder.

"The term *evil* has a certain political incorrectness attached to it since we now have open communications channels and temporary alliances with some factions of the supernatural community."

Community, ha! She made a face at her own

cautious language. She thoroughly disliked assigning such things as culture and cohesion to the obvious bad guys, but that was the way vampires and other monsters were defined these days. Mainly because they didn't often cause trouble in the modern world. Heck, she had to admit that serial killers took out far more people than vampire attacks in any given year. But that didn't mean that death by preternatural blood-draining monsters wasn't still a possibility that needed to be guarded against.

"The Clan Primes have agreed to a mutual investigation of Tribe activities with the hunters. This preliminary investigation is to be carried out by me and a Prime of the Wolf Clan."

Eden looked at her watch, then down at the entrance to the alley three floors below. Not a shadow was moving down there. She didn't see anything when she checked with her night-vision lenses, either.

He was late.

She hoped this Clan guy wasn't planning on making some sort of dramatic entrance; she was *so* not in the mood.

She moved to the front of the roof and saw nothing but light traffic on the street; no pedestrians. She sighed and checked the other side again.

Finally there was someone down there. She couldn't make out details from this distance, even with the night-vision glasses, but her specialized equipment registered that he was a vampire. He was walking slowly, carefully checking his surroundings, and she approved of his caution. It told her that even the legendarily arrogant, superpowered Primes weren't completely stupid when it came to undercover work.

Her moment of admiration evaporated when she saw that the vampire wasn't alone. The pair that followed him were also vampires.

Damn it, the deal was for a human and a vampire to work together. Had she fallen for a trap? Then the lone vampire stopped and turned, and the others rushed toward him. They had to be Tribe Primes pulling an ambush; they'd somehow found out about the meeting.

She saw their movements as streaks of light through the goggles. The action was too swift for human eyes to follow, but there was definitely a fight going on—and the odds were not in favor of her Clan contact.

"Oh no, you don't!" Eden proclaimed. "That's *my* vampire!"

She snatched up her crossbow and ran for the fire escape.

*　　*　　*

"Ow!"

One of the bastards was carrying a Taser. Laurent backed up and kicked the shock weapon out of the guy's hand. As he did, the other one came up behind him and got an arm around Laurent's throat.

He'd let them chase him into an alley, which was bloody stupid of him. The whole time they were physically on him, they were also psychically attacking him, sending images at him, trying to confuse him. It wasn't working, but it was annoying. Though maybe it was working a little, as he was imagining a shadow racing down a nearby fire escape.

Laurent buried his fangs deep into the arm at his throat. This managed to loosen the grip so that he could slip through and drop to the ground. From there he was able to shoulder-roll away from the pair.

Before he could spring back to his feet, someone behind him yelled "Down!"

The projectile that flashed past barely missed him. Laurent heard the thud of impact and looked up just as one of his attackers fell to the ground, an arrow sticking out of his chest. Shot in the heart, Laurent realized.

If there was one thing instantly fatal to a vampire—or anyone, come to think of it—it was having the heart pierced by a sharp wooden object.

The other attacker took one look at his dead friend and ran. Laurent was tempted to do the same. But he remembered that he'd been warned, so he rose to his feet and carefully turned to face his rescuer.

"Thanks," he said to the tall mortal woman standing beneath the streetlight.

"You're late," she answered.

He never argued with a woman holding a crossbow. "Sorry."

The other attacker didn't argue, either. He pelted off when the woman stepped forward.

As she walked toward him, Laurent noticed that the mortal was attractive in a sharp-featured way. He liked her long legs, but not her very short hair. Not that this was a good time to take inventory of her womanly charms. She was the one holding the weapon, and he didn't know why she'd helped him. She certainly didn't give off any friendly vibes.

"You do know you killed somebody?" he questioned as she came to stand over the body.

She gave him a scathing look. "Like you've never killed anyone, Wolf."

He hadn't, and he wasn't named Wolf. He almost informed her of her mistake, but then he

recalled that Clan Wolf were the dominant vampires in the area. So—she thought he was a Clan
boy, did she? He didn't suppose this was any
time to be offended by the mistake.

"Oh, right, vampires don't like to kill other
vampires." She gave him a mocking smile.
"Don't worry. I'll protect you."

Did she have any idea how dangerous it was
to speak to a Tribe Prime like that? Especially
for a woman? He looked her up and down with
cold, assessing arrogance.

While she ignored him and spoke into a cell
phone. "Bring a body bag. I've got a pickup."

Laurent looked on with a sudden admiration
for the human hunter's efficiency. This woman
had an infrastructure. She had backup. She
thought he was here to help her.

She had no idea how much trouble she was
in.

When she got off the phone, he smiled at her
with all the charisma Primes were born with,
which he'd honed to survive.

"Can I buy you a cup of coffee, Ms.—"

Chapter Two

"Faveau," she answered, and felt herself growing warm from the intensity of his gaze. It was a vampire thing, she remembered; nothing personal. And she'd been trained to fight off the creature's hypnotic stare.

But he was the most gorgeous male she'd ever seen. His voice was so deep and delicious that one word shook her down to her toes. She forced herself to look away, took a few deep breaths, and irritation returned as she looked back at him.

"Eden Faveau," she reminded him. "I was told you'd be briefed on this assignment."

He shrugged. It was an elegant, altogether disarming gesture. "Sorry." After a moment's hesitation, he added, "There wasn't time."

He was magnificent, with those big eyes and sharp cheekbones and long platinum blond hair pulled back in a thick braid. She was going to have to stay annoyed at him as a shield against his preternatural beauty and psychic gifts.

"Here's your briefing," she snapped. "You, Sid Wolf. Me, Eden Faveau. We work together—"

"Why?"

"I'm getting to that."

"Couldn't we do this over coffee? I really don't like conversations over rotting corpses. It's so—"

"Vampiric?"

"Stereotypically so." Suddenly he was standing at her side, with a hand on her elbow. He urged her forward. "Let's get to know each other somewhere more civilized."

She wasn't interested in knowing him—but this place *would* look like a crime scene to any hapless human that showed up before the cleanup squad. It was best that she and Wolf not remain with the body.

"Most of my equipment's up on the roof." She made an effort to move away.

Wolf released her. "Wait here."

Before she could move, he was gone. She caught a blur as he raced up the fire escape. Within moments he was back down, carrying her gear.

"It looks like having a vampire around might come in handy."

"You have no idea."

She hadn't meant to speak out loud. She put the slip of the tongue down to having spent time talking into a tape recorder recently. It *was* possible that the vampire had plucked the words directly from her mind, even though she'd been told that Clan vampires were careful about mental intrusions.

"You're standing there looking like I'm going to eat you," he said. "Which I never do on a first date." He gestured again. "Shall we go?"

"This is not a *date*."

He sighed. "Listen, I know you vampire hunters have your sense of humor surgically removed, but mine is intact, and I like to use it in conversations. Bear with me, okay?"

She did so have a sense of humor! But she'd just killed a sentient being, and was having a little trouble dealing with it. If she kept up the hard-ass routine and kept telling herself that was a monster lying on the ground, she could get through the night, and maybe do it again if she had to. And with this gorgeous creature in front of her threatening to cloud her reason with his beauty, and making wisecracks besides—

what she needed to do was turn off her emotions altogether, and get on with the job.

"Coffee," she said. "Fine."

Laurent looked at the frothy mocha drink cradled in Eden Faveau's hands with the same distaste she would have given to him sipping on a pint of warm blood. He liked her hands even if he didn't approve of her taste. They looked strong and capable, unadorned by any jewelry. She wore plain black clothing, appropriate for commando ops on evil vampires. He studied her in the bright light of the small coffee shop and found her—austere. She had the sort of strong, noble features better suited to a statue of Athena than to the modern world. Hers was not a soft beauty.

Having her would be more of a conquest than a seduction. And wouldn't that be a delight?

"What are you looking at?" she demanded.

"Your nose."

Eden wished she hadn't asked. It was bad enough the vampire was prettier than she was; did he have to insult her about it, too?

"What about my nose?"

"I like it." He reached across the narrow table and touched the tip of it. "I like it a lot."

What on earth was there to like about her nose? "It's large."

"No. Long, yes, but elegant."

Eden didn't think he was insulting her; he seemed to be giving an honest opinion. Or at least, he was flattering her in a way meant to be disarming, and it almost worked. There was something inside her that wanted to preen and ask what else he liked. She shook her head, more disgusted with herself than him.

"I've been living in Los Angeles the last few decades, and most of the women there are at least one-quarter plastic. It's nice to see someone with all her original equipment."

His gaze slid lower.

It wasn't like she was dressed for seduction, but the black knit shirt she was wearing did outline her breasts.

"Nicely original," he murmured.

"How can you tell?" she asked, curiosity pummeling down any sense of outrage. "X-ray vision?"

"More of a heat-seeking sense."

Of course he meant that he was aware of the blood flowing through her body. You couldn't squeeze blood from silicone any more than you could from a turnip, she supposed. So of course he could tell that she was all natural. And what odd tangents the brain went off on when facing a vampire across a coffee-shop table.

"I thought the Jackals ran L.A.," she said, trying to get back on track, or at least gather some intel.

He quirked an eyebrow. "Jackals? My dear, they call themselves Clan Shagal. That's jackal in Persian, I think. Very high-class, the Shagals. I've been hanging with them lately, and they're so noble and pure I was nearly bored to death."

Eden was shocked at the vampire's assessment of his own kind. "You're not noble and pure?"

There was a wicked gleam in his eye when he answered. "I said *they* were boring. Being good all the time seems to come easy for them."

"But not for you?"

"I am not a perfect man. Of course, I'm not a man at all. Exactly. By your definition. Though my equipment *is* in perfect working order."

He gave her a devilish grin that almost made her think he was cute, rather than incorrigible. But she couldn't forget he was a predator. And her kind were the preferred prey.

"You only look human," she told him.

"You do know that there's a belief among the Clans that your kind and mine are the same species, separated by minor mutations? And that it is the duty of the more advanced types to protect their little brothers and sisters?" He snorted. "No, really. They believe that."

Eden laughed. "Mutants protecting regular folks? You people believe you're the X-Men? Would that make you Wolverine?"

He reached across the narrow table to touch the tip of her nose. "Madam, it is not your sarcasm I mind. It is your choice of mutant. I would obviously be Gambit."

It surprised her that the vampire's touch was warm and gentle. It also surprised her that he'd just mentioned her favorite comic-book character—Remy LeBeau, aka Gambit, a thief, a rogue, a man deeply in love with a woman he could never touch, and full of guilt for crimes he'd committed while working for a man he didn't know was a supervillain. Ah, Gambit!

"He's your favorite, too!" the vampire said, drawing his hand away. And looking smug. "Wouldn't I be perfect to play him in the movie?"

"You don't look a thing like him. Besides, the movie Rogue is still too young to meet Gambit." And why was she talking about movies and comic-book heroes with the creature she was assigned to work with? She did not want to know that they had things in common. It made him seem more like a person than a simulacrum of humanity.

She straightened stiffly in her chair. "Humans don't need your protection. But for our mutual benefit, we acknowledge that we occasionally need your help."

"Did you rehearse that?"

"Yes. It was part of *my* briefing."

He spread his hands out before him. Elegant, long-fingered pale hands.

She wanted those hands on her.

Damn!

"I didn't miss the briefing on purpose." He laid his palms flat on the table and took a dramatic look around the coffee shop. They were the only ones there. "Talk to me," he urged. "Tell me everything." He checked his watch. "And soon. The night's not exactly young, darling."

Fortunately his smart-ass attitude nicely counteracted his amazing looks. Eden gritted her teeth at the *darling*.

She did take the time to finish the last few sips of her mocha latte, showing that she didn't take orders from him. Maybe it was childish, but she had to do something to keep the balance of power tilted toward the human side.

"All right," she said after patting her lips

with a napkin. "There's been an influx of Tribe vampires into the San Diego area recently."

"I've noticed that."

"We've been trying to keep tabs on them, make sure they don't do anything illegal. Your side has been trying to find out what makes our fair city so interesting all of a sudden."

"Well, it can't be for the desert sunshine," he said. "Not for Tribe types."

"That's what we thought. After all, everybody knows that the Tribes don't use those daylight drugs of yours. And why is that?" she wondered. "If everyone else uses them, why don't the Tribes?"

"Not every Clan or Family vampire uses them," he told her. "For one thing the king Primes among the Tribes forbid their use. For another, the Clans control access to the drugs. There's too much baggage that comes along with a Tribe Prime coming in from the dark. If a Tribe member is willing to renounce his culture and history, and whole way of life, then the Clan scientists might let him use the drugs. *After* he's been reeducated and proved his worthiness to be adopted into a Family. Or if he grovels enough, he might even"—he gave a mocking gasp and put his hand over his heart—"be allowed to serve one of the high and mighty

Clans." He sounded even more bitter when he added, "There's a long waiting list to abandon the Tribe way of life. Of course, if the pack leaders find any of these traitors, the poor bastards are executed in gruesome, horrible, and really fun for the rest of the pack ways."

Eden folded her hands on the black marble tabletop and stared at the vampire. It surprised her that he didn't sound like he approved of his own kind's policy of screening the candidates who tried to escape from Tribe life. Of course, they were all still vampires no matter what their affiliation. But the Clans did have a better track record for blending into the modern world.

Or maybe they were just better at hiding their crimes against humanity. The hunters didn't have strong evidence of overt evil, so they kept truce with the Clans, and mostly with the Families. The Tribes were fair game, and the Tribes were the problem right now.

"I notice you didn't mention anything about Tribe females changing sides," she said.

For a long, dangerous moment he looked at her like he thought she was crazy. In fact, there was a smoldering outrage in his eyes that frightened her.

Then he blinked and smiled faintly. "We don't know much about Tribe females."

Eden suspected this was a lie, but let it go. Gaining insights into vampire society was fascinating, but it wasn't worth alienating her partner just because they were touchy about their females.

She couldn't blame the Prime for his attitude. Once upon a time, human hunters had made a concerted effort to kill all vampire females. The reasoning was that if they couldn't breed, the monsters would die out. The monsters didn't take kindly to this attempt at genocide, and the resulting war had been devastating on vampires and hunters alike. It was one of the few times all three types of vampires had joined forces to work together. Though this had been back long, long ago, in the 1300s, Eden suspected the vampires still held a grudge. Heck, as long-lived as the vampires were, Wolf might have had close relatives involved in the conflict.

"How old are you?" she asked him.

"Do you know the Police song 'Born in the Fifties'?" he answered.

"Who are the Police?"

He sighed. "What passes for music these days . . . Let's just say I'm not quite old enough to collect Social Security. No, I'm lying," he added, and looked startled at the admission. "I'm older than that. It comes from living in Los

Angeles where youth really matters." He tilted his head to one side and gave her another thorough looking-over. "I never ask a lady her age." He grinned. "But I'm good at guessing."

Eden almost didn't hear what he said; she was trying too hard to control the wave of sensual heat sweeping through her. It didn't get any better when he took her hand and ran his thumb in a slow sweep over her palm. Her breathing became ragged and the whole world centered around the point where skin met skin.

"You see, this is the sort of thing you should not let a Prime do," he said. And broke the spell by taking his hand away. "Not during business hours, at least."

Her flush of desire turned to one of embarrassment. "Lesson learned," she gritted between clenched teeth.

He gave a brisk nod. "Don't worry, Faveau, we'll get each other trained. This is my first assignment, too."

She hadn't said anything about this being her first assignment, but she let it go.

"I've never worked with humans before, but I do have plenty of experience on the streets," he reassured her. "What are the Tribe boys doing that has the hunters working with the Clans?"

Eden blamed herself for getting so off track.

So she straightened in the chair and spoke quickly. "There's a drug known as Dawn. It's a knockoff of your daylight drugs. We don't know who is making it, or who is distributing it to the Tribe primes, but San Diego is the source. That's why the sudden influx of vampires into the city."

"Dawn?" His eyes lit with interest, when righteous indignation would have been more reassuring. "A way to bypass the strictures of the Clans and the Tribes."

"It's dangerous for them."

He nodded. "But I can see why they'd risk it for a shot at a daylight life."

"No. I mean it's *dangerous* for them. And for us. There are psychotic side effects. After taking Dawn for a while, they go nuts. Like that pair that attacked you."

Chapter Three

Laurent almost laughed at the notion that Tribe Primes ever *needed* a reason to attack. He doubted this rip-off drug could cause his Tribe brethren to behave psychotically; Dawn probably just gave them more waking hours to be themselves.

And he wasn't here to help Eden, even if her earnestness almost made him forget himself for a few minutes. He was Laurent of the Manticores, merely pretending to be of the pure-hearted, noble Clan Wolf.

And he wasn't even *exactly* pretending. She'd seen a vampire being attacked by other vampires, and made a rash assumption. The mistake was hers.

This arrogant female would pay for her mistake when he gave in to his strong natural desire to taste both her blood and her body. Arousal sparked off her, and he savored the tension of fighting his own response.

There was a part of him that almost wanted to protect Eden Faveau from her mistake. But she'd killed a vampire right before his eyes. She'd saved his life, but she'd killed one of his kind to do it. His gratitude was mixed with wariness, when he should have nothing but contempt for this human.

Okay, he *might* have killed the guy himself, but that was his right as a Prime fighting another Prime.

She was a female, a soft creature of warm flesh and hot blood meant for use. She needed him, as a partner and ally, and his reaction to that disturbed him. He could make women want him, but need in any way was new, different— nice.

"Oh, hell," he muttered.

He'd definitely spent too much time in the presence of Clan boys lately; all that concentrated nobility must have messed with his head. But his time among the Jackals, Foxes, and Crows had also taught him how to *act* like one of them. And maybe some insight into this Dawn drug.

He almost opened his mouth to tell her, but luckily she interrupted this idiocy.

"Hell what?" she asked.

"Nothing."

"But—"

He waved away the question and rose to his feet. He was here to use her, and it was time they got going—before the real Sid Wolf showed up to complicate Laurent's life even further.

He pulled back her chair to help her stand, which seemed like a gallant Clan sort of gesture. She brushed against him as she got up, and the contact stunned him. He became almost painfully aware of her warmth, and of her scent. His arm came around her waist, and he pulled her against him before he could think about it.

"What the hell—!"

She struggled, and that woke up his need to hunt, control, and dominate. Oh, yeah, he was Tribe all right! The elbow she jammed sharply into his stomach would have brought him back to his senses, but Laurent had already felt the presence of the others a moment before the pain registered.

"We've got company," he whispered in her ear. "Time to leave."

The woman immediately became alert to the danger, all business. "How many? Where? How did they find us?"

He was aware of her annoyance at herself for

asking a question she knew wasn't necessary to their immediate problem, but this was the question he chose to answer. Just not necessarily truthfully.

"The one that got away must have picked up your scent. They'll want revenge for the one you killed," he said, providing only half an answer.

Or at least not completely accurate. They might be after her, too. Revenge was a big part of Tribe culture.

"Me?"

He kept his arm around her waist as he considered possibilities, and felt her start of surprise. "Don't worry, partner. We'll be fine." If he told her he'd protect her, he'd likely get an elbow in the stomach again. He concentrated for a moment. "Two, maybe three in the parking lot."

"Then I guess we go out the back door."

"When you said we'd go out the back, I thought you wanted to leave."

She'd insisted that they do a little recon. Eden looked at her vampire companion. "Most of my equipment's in my car."

"You can come back for it later."

"I want my car."

They were crouched on the roof of the coffee

shop, looking down on the parking lot of the small strip mall.

"There are three vampires down there."

"Do they know we're up here?"

She watched Wolf close his eyes and concentrate. He looked like a radiant angel when the frustration left his features, though Eden figured the radiant part might have something to do with how his pale skin looked in the moonlight. She didn't know why he was being so willing to run away.

All right, so she agreed with his *"Live to fight another day"* argument. But she didn't like the thought of having those *things* on her tail. She didn't have any psychic talents to help her detect their presence. All she had was her wits, her training, her stuff—and him.

"Well?" she asked Wolf.

He opened his eyes. "You could call for backup."

"You're my—"

"I knew you were going to say that." He looked back down at the lot as a car pulled in. Another car pulled out. "One of the reasons they haven't attacked us yet is because this area is busy."

"There's an all-night pharmacy, the convenience store, and the coffee shop." She glanced at the sky. "Maybe the concentration of traffic will keep us safe until sunrise."

He also looked up at the sky. "If they're using the drug, sunrise isn't going to be *their* problem."

He sounded worried. "Whose problem will it be?" she asked suspiciously.

"You could call your friends from earlier tonight," he suggested. "Strength in numbers, and all that."

She sighed. "They're busy. Besides, I'm supposed to be working with you. The fewer people involved in an operation the better."

"Why?" He suddenly looked disgusted. "Don't tell me you hunters play by the same sort of outmoded stupid rules that hog-tie the Clans *and* the Tribes?" His hand landed on her shoulder. "Why, oh why, can't we all forget about the past and behave sensibly? Just once?"

She shrugged away from his touch. Even if she did see his point, she was still appalled—in a knee jerk sort of way—to hear a vampire Prime speaking like this.

"What's the matter with you? I thought the Clans were supposed to hate the Tribes as much as we do. What are you doing here if—"

"Maybe they sent someone who doesn't feel

rabid, fanatical hatred for anyone," he snarled at her.

His eyes were glowing. It was enough to make the hairs on the back of her neck stand on end. Eden was slowly reaching for the garlic spray in her pocket when Wolf got himself under control.

"I'm a peaceful kind of guy," he asserted. "Live and let live, I say. Except when terminating with extreme prejudice is absolutely called for."

She glanced down at the parking lot. "Like now?"

"No."

"Fine. I'll do it."

She stood up. He dragged her back down. She was surprised by the lack of effort it took him. She knew vampires were stronger and faster than humans, but personally experiencing the results of these heightened senses was a much more visceral experience. She'd have to remember to mention that in her audiotape report.

But first they had to get out of here. "You're supposed to be helping me," she reminded him. "Are you afraid of the odds?"

"Afraid?"

This time he was the one who surged to his feet, but Eden didn't try to stop him. He practically vibrated with indignation and gave her a look so haughty it was blood-chilling.

The next instant, he leapt off the roof into the center of the busy mall lot, landing on the roof of an SUV. Then he jumped again, landing on the vampire sitting on the hood of her car. She could hear the sound of bones breaking from up here—and hoped they weren't Wolf's.

"One down," he called up to her.

She saw two shadows rushing toward him, and rushed to the ladder behind the building. While she ran around to the front of the mall, she heard honking and shouting and the crash of glass and metal.

"So much for discretion," she murmured.

He was causing a hell of a scene. She was sure that cell phones had been popped out by now and that the cops had been called. There were witnesses to a weird, high-speed brawl. This was not the way the night games were supposed to be played; there were rules. Centuries-old rules. Everybody—vampires and hunters included— had a tacit understanding that it was safer for the general population to keep the supernatural side of the world carefully hidden away.

Wolf was opening her car door when she dashed across the lot to his side. He barely looked mussed.

She looked around frantically. There were humans gaping at them from inside their vehicles and at the doors of the stores, but she didn't see any of Tribe Primes.

"They took their wounded and left," he said. Then he grinned. "Truth is, they ran when all the noise started. Sometimes breaking the rules is the only way to solve a problem," he added before she could point out what he'd done. "Get in the car. Wait," he added.

Then he grabbed her and kissed her before she knew what was happening. His mouth was hard on hers, and his tongue demanding. She felt like a match being struck. All she could do was tilt her head back against his arm and ride the sudden blaze.

It was over in a moment.

He stepped back, and said "Shall I drive?" cool and calm as you please.

Eden had to lean against the car, too full of heat and confusion to think for a few moments. She finally managed to lift her head and angrily demand, "What was that about?"

Wolf was totally insouciant, totally unashamed. "That's one of the old rules, isn't it? That the hero gets to kiss the girl he just saved."

She made a dramatic gesture of wiping the

back of her hand across her mouth. "You didn't save me."

"I saved your car."

"Then kiss the car."

"I'd rather drive."

"No." She slid past him into the front seat. She had the car started and in gear by the time he got into the passenger's seat. "Fasten your seat belt." She hated that desire seethed in her as much as anger, and her voice sounded rough with emotion. "Where to?"

"Somewhere dark."

"Couldn't we start following what few leads I have?"

"I need some rest. It's near daylight," he added.

"Couldn't I just drop you at your place?"

"Of course not. No way I'm going to be tracked home by crazed Dawn addicts. You shouldn't return to your home, either. You do have a warded safe house set up for this operation, right?"

She did, but she was reluctant to bring a vampire who had just kissed her there. "Why do you need somewhere dark to rest?" she asked suspiciously.

"Because I don't use the daylight drugs."

She'd suspected as much. "Damn."

"Sorry if it inconveniences you."

"Inconveniences me? If you can't go out in the light, how much help are you going to be to this operation?"

"I work by night just fine."

At least she didn't hear any double entendres in his tone. In fact, he sounded bone-weary. And she supposed arguing with him about his lifestyle choice wasn't going to do them any good.

She knew from reading intelligence reports that taking the drugs or not was a choice each Clan and Family vampire made for themselves. There was still controversy and dissent among the vampires about the daylight drugs, even though they'd been available for decades. Some of the vampires didn't think the cocktail of chemicals was safe. Some thought they changed the fundamental nature of what it meant to be a vampire. Some were just old-fashioned.

The other cars had left the lot, and she thought she heard police sirens in the distance. The time for their getaway was almost overdue. At the mall entrance she paused for a moment to look around. She saw no vampires, cops, or civilians. The only creature in sight was a huge black dog sitting beneath a streetlamp. It turned its head to watch her as she took a right and drove quickly away.

Interesting, Joe thought as the vampire hunter drove off. The woman was alert and had even noticed him, but the vampire with her was already napping. He took a moment to scratch behind his ear, then he stood, stretched, and took a long, deep sniff of air. Exhaust fumes were the dominant scent, but he was used to that. The evening air in the city was rife with many other aromas. He could stand here breathing it all in and analyzing for hours, but werewolves who gave in to that temptation in busy urban areas tended to end up in the pound.

And it was embarrassing to have to be rescued by one's relatives. It had happened before, though not to him. The possibility of needing aid was the reason he often left his clothes in a safe hiding place, but he always wore a gold chain with a cartouche-shaped medallion etched with his name and a phone number around his neck.

There were a great many vampires in town at the moment, not all of them friendlies. In fact, most were the sort that smelled bad. It was a psychic aura more than a physical scent, but the result still left a nasty residue on werewolf senses. Joe wondered if the vampires knew that each type had their own distinct scent. From in-breeding, he supposed.

It was similar with the human hunters. It hadn't taken him long to sniff out the essence that marked her kind. It was nice to discover that she'd hooked up with a competent Clan Prime.

The one with the human hunter smelled like a Wolf, mostly. There was a hint of something else clinging to the Prime. But he'd been in a fight with the Tribe boys, so it was possible that he had some Tribe scent on him left over from the scuffle.

All Joe knew for certain was that the vampire was not Sid Wolf. But that was all right. He'd been concerned Sid would get involved in some-thing that wasn't company business when they were so shorthanded. He'd wanted to make sure that wasn't the case, so he could talk Sid out of it if he had to.

Joe figured that Sid had called in a cousin to work on this assignment. Joe didn't want his partner to have anything to do with this drug case, even if Sid was all into this Clan honor stuff.

He was satisfied that the situation was cov-ered. Sid would show up at the office of Bleythin Investigations on Monday morning, and they could get back to working missing-persons cases.

Joe yawned and trotted back toward where he'd parked his car. Being in wolf form took a lot of energy, and it had been a long night for him, too. It was time for him to go home and get some sleep.

Chapter Four

"Come here, little girl."

She threw a lamp at him, plunging the room into darkness.

"You forget that I can see in the dark?"

"Don't come near me!"

She was pressed up against a wall of the windowless room. There was a bed between them, but the door was to his back. There was no way she was getting out. The only place she was going was on her back, with him on top of her. In her. That was going to be sweet. But he was going to play for a while first. It had been a long time since he'd been completely in control. He wanted her body and her blood, but breaking her spirit was going to come first.

"Blood slave," he said. "You know the term. I'm going to make you mine." He held up a hand. "Please don't tell me you'd rather die first."

"I don't do clichés," she answered, as she looked around for anything to use as a weapon.

"You're a killer," he reminded her. "You're going to pay for that."

He was on her in the next heartbeat. He felt her heart beneath his hand, felt its hard, frantic flutter under soft skin and fragile bone. Blood drove through it in a panicked rush. Her fear was a sweet tangy scent, better than perfume, better than anything—but blood. And sex.

"Eden," he said, and stroked her short hair before running his claws ever so gently down her throat and over her breasts. He ripped her shirt to shreds but left no mark on her. But the fear of what he could do marked her soul, and it was delicious.

He licked his lips, then her throat. He tasted the salt of sweat and savored the heat of her skin and her pulse under his tongue. He let his fangs grow hard, slowly pierced fear-heated flesh, licked the wound, then suckled. Her body arched against his, helpless against the pleasure. She moaned, low and frantic. He laughed, forcing the sound into her mind, knowing that she hated what he made her feel.

"It's only going to get worse," he told her, and laid her on the bed.

He didn't taste her again. In fact, he let the

blood desire die down before he touched her
again. When he slid his hands over her, it was as
a man touching a woman. He luxuriated in the
feel of warm, smooth skin, of curves and shadows, the play of muscle. He took in scent and
texture. Everything he did was to please himself.
She belonged to him, and it pleased him to learn
every inch of what was his. If he used his skill to
arouse—well, that was her problem to deal
with. It didn't matter to him if her body wanted
what her mind hated.

Her hatred was an aphrodisiac.

When he almost couldn't hold on anymore,
he bit into his wrist. When the blood was flowing, he held her head to the small wound and
wouldn't let her go until he was sure she'd swal-
lowed a few drops. Only a little for now, just
enough to start the craving.

When she gasped from the new fire running
through her, he pushed her back on the bed and
entered her. He drove into her hard and fast,
making sure she knew it was his cock she
served.

For now.

Forever.

Laurent woke hard as a rock, and with a
headache that felt like somebody had just

dropped a ton of lava into his head. He felt around quickly, finding the bed empty. He could barely lift his head to look, but the room was empty as well.

Thank God for that!

It had only been a dream. Some horrible nightmare. One that left him aroused and covered in sweat. He flopped back down on the pillow, eyes tightly shut. The pain in his head was so bad, he wasn't sure if he was even up to jacking off. He took deep, steady breaths, working to get his body calm and his head clear.

What had *that* been about? Eden Faveau hadn't pissed him off enough for him to want to play those kind of games with her. Sex, yeah, but rape—?

But wasn't that what he was supposed to want—a harem of devoted blood slaves? That shouldn't have been a nightmare; it was supposed to be every Tribe Prime's fondest dream. That kind of rape was what he *should* fantasize about. Instead, he woke up frightened and disgusted.

Justinian was right. He didn't have what it took to be a Prime.

Laurent snarled into the darkness, hating the pack leader who might be his sire. And hating himself.

Or maybe it was the headache he hated. His ability to self-heal was toning the pain down, but it wasn't completely going away. What was with that?

His senses told him it was midday, but a heavy curtain covered the bedroom's small window. So it wasn't sunlight causing the pain. Of course, there was silver, garlic, and hawthorn wood placed all over the small apartment. He had allergies to all of them, and other various herbs and stuff. The concentration of substances might be the problem, added to the fact that he couldn't remember the last time he'd gotten any real rest. Vampires didn't need to sleep often, but when they did . . .

"What the—?" he muttered at the sound of a voice coming from the living room, just as he was about to fall back asleep.

He sensed only Eden in the place, so she must be on the phone. Laurent scrubbed his hands over his face and concentrated. Even with the headache and several doors between them, his hearing was good enough to make out Eden's voice if he tried.

"—don't think the local vampire community is taking the threat seriously. Or maybe it's a lack of respect for us. How are we supposed to work on this case twenty-four/seven"—she paused to yawn—"if the Prime assigned to it doesn't even take the daylight drugs? And does that pose a security risk? We've assumed that use of the drugs tones down the vampire's natural violent tendencies. Still, I have to admit that I have yet to see any unstable or violent tendencies exhibited by Wolf. I'm the one who insisted he attack the Tribe members in the parking lot; he was in favor of a strategic retreat. When he did use force, it was quite efficient, but flashy. He drew attention to our presence. They're not supposed to do that."

She paused.

By this time Laurent had figured out that his human partner was dictating some sort of report. He started to doze off again.

Then she said, "He kissed me. I liked it."

Of course you did. He smiled. Maybe he should do it again. He remembered his dream and shook his head. Though he planned on seducing her, now wasn't the best time.

"I suppose the reaction was telepathically induced."

It was not!

"But since I have no psychic talent, the effect was not as strong as it would have been on someone gifted. Knowing his seductive abilities will help arm me against them in the future."

Sweetheart, you ain't seen nothing yet.

"He isn't what I thought a vampire would be like. For one thing, he seems to have some sympathy for the Tribe members that are using Dawn. He almost made me see that they have a point of view. And one should never look at the world from the monster's point of view."

Yeah, if you do that you might not see them as monsters anymore. Of course, we are monsters, but we have a point of view.

"He doesn't behave in the way I've been briefed that a Clan Prime would act."

I'll have to work on that.

"He's not particularly haughty or arrogant or insistent on everything being done his way. There are flashes of machismo, but they're leavened with humor. One of the things that disturbs me is how much I enjoyed talking to him. He's—quirky."

Quirky? What the hell kind of way is that to describe a Prime? Madam, I am evil.

"I'm not sure if that's good or bad. Bad, if it impacts the case. Bad for me even if it doesn't, because I'm always attracted to quirky. I'll have to work harder to keep my distance. That will mean concentrating more on resisting him, when all my attention should be on the job."

She sighed, and he heard the tape rewinding.

Apparently Eden was preparing to start over with a bit less personal commentary.

"The zapper is running at full strength," she began.

He had no idea what this meant, and didn't care. He went back to sleep, resisting the temptation to eavesdrop by putting a pillow over his head.

"I learned how to pick the lock," he said.

The beautiful woman turned around and smiled, though her gaze went worriedly to the door before it returned to him. She'd been cupping the heavy glass paperweight she'd told him came from Venice. She said it came from a before time and was her favorite thing, but for him.

She put it down and held out her arms, and he rushed into them. "Laurent, my little wolf cub."

Her embrace was strong and warm, and she smelled wonderful. She was careful to keep the silver chains binding her from touching him. She had always worn the chains; they were a part of her. When he'd asked her about the pain, she'd laughed. The sound had been as light as a feather, but he'd known it was false.

Her cell was the only place where the world

even pretended to be safe. The room contained an ornate bed and too many windows. It was almost dark now, so it wasn't too hard to be here. His eyes ached and his skin itched, but it was safer to be here now than in true darkness.

While he liked being held by her, he wriggled free. "I've learned how to pick locks."

She cupped his chin. Her gentleness made him shiver. "A useful skill. Perhaps not honorable, but useful. How do you plan on using this skill, cub?"

"To undo your chains," he answered.

"The silver would hurt you."

"I don't mind."

She looked at him steadily for a moment. Her eyes were so calm, so beautiful. So was her touch on his mind. She nodded finally. "You are brave."

He needed to help her. "Please."

"Perhaps I will let you—"

Then the door he'd carefully closed crashed open. She gasped, and tried to hide him behind her. Justinian laughed at her effort and pulled them apart. Laurent landed hard on the floor, and it was a long way to look up at the pack leader. But for a hard kick that knocked the breath from him, Justinian ignored him.

"Antonia, I am going to miss you," Justinian

said. "But times are hard for my little pack. We have to run again, and you're financing the move." He ran his hands over her, and pulled her up so he could take a quick taste from her throat. "I've found a buyer for you." Justinian looked down to where he cowered. "Perhaps you'll breed better for your new master than you have for me."

The headache woke Laurent once more, but the ache this time was far more than physical.

In the dream he was always helpless. In reality, he'd thrown himself on Justinian and gotten the beating of his life for it.

Justinian had been an excellent teacher.

But Laurent wasn't going to think about that right now. "Maybe tomorrow," he muttered, and got out of bed.

Chapter Five

She was asleep. Wearing a sports bra and underwear. Her tanned skin looked glorious against the pale pink sheets. The round curves of her breasts and hips were pretty glorious, too. Laurent stood in the doorway of the apartment's other bedroom and resented the peaceful expression on the human's face. She was all loose-limbed and relaxed, obviously not afflicted with bad dreams. The unfairness was enough to make his fangs ache.

It annoyed him that she felt so safe being alone with a vampire, even if she did think he was one of the good guys. In his experience, even the good guys weren't all that good. They were as continually hot and horny as any other kind of Prime. Maybe with better impulse control. But he'd heard plenty of stories of Clan and Family Primes taking what they wanted and justifying it later with all the bondmate crap.

I don't have to pretend to be civilized, he thought, wanting her.

Eden Faveau was not conventionally beautiful, but he liked what he saw. She would take some taming, but—

No! You tamed the ones you kept. He'd never been interested in that sort of thing; use 'em and move on was his lifestyle. Traveling light was safe and sensible—it was survival.

But maybe once he got Justinian off his back . . .

What, he could lead a normal life? As what?

He wasn't used to being so trapped with his own thoughts. Come to think of it, he wasn't used to having a headache, either. He was willing to bet the two were related. And that the human woman he was standing here *yearning* over was somehow responsible.

He strode forward and grasped Eden by the shoulder.

There was an angel leaning over her. Long silver hair flowed over his broad shoulders, and there was a light of righteous fury in his gray eyes. Eden stared at this vision in wonder, not sure who he was or where she was.

All she knew was that he was beautiful and—
"Wha—?" she asked.

Then she recognized Wolf, and remembered that she'd dragged herself to bed sometime in the middle of the afternoon after being up for nearly two days. She'd been asleep, and it was good. He'd woken her up. They were both dressed only in their underwear. That was as far as logic would go at the moment.

"Wolf." She looked past his broad shoulders. "What are you doing in my room?"

"What are you doing to me?" he demanded.

Huh? She'd been dreaming about doing some things with him, but she didn't think that's what he was talking about. 'Cause he didn't look turned on, he looked pissed off.

With no effort at all he pulled her to her feet. "Why does my head hurt?"

"Your head hurts?"

She had no idea. After all, he was a vampire, and they didn't get sick like real people. Their bodies and their minds were different, and—

Brains. Brain waves.

"Oh," she said, finally coming fully awake. "Sorry. It must be the zapper. I didn't think how it might affect you." He was glaring at her in a way that left her hot and flustered, and she was very aware of hands like velvet over titanium holding her arms. "It's an electrical device meant to keep vampires out. I'll go turn it off."

He released her. "You do that."

She hurried into the living room with the vampire following after. A large array of computers and surveillance equipment took up much of the room. There was a couch against one wall and a small dining table next to the entrance to the galley kitchen.

Eden sat down and typed instructions on a keyboard, then flipped a couple of switches. Then she turned back to the vampire who was standing tensely in the middle of the room. After a few seconds, he visibly relaxed.

"Better?" she asked.

He rubbed his forehead, then nodded. "Don't do that again." He sighed and pulled his hair away from his face. "Coffee," he said. "Blood."

"There's blood in the fridge," she answered.

"Human?"

"No way."

He sighed again. "You could get volunteers, you know. Or get it from a blood bank."

"You could provide your own," she suggested. "We were just trying to be polite to an ally."

"If you *really* want to be polite . . ."

He eyed her up and down, making her suddenly very nervous. But there was also something in his hot glance that made her nipples go hard, and fire shot through her. Along with an image of her lying beneath his hard weight on the floor, arching in pleasure as fangs sank deep into her flesh.

He took a step toward her and ran his tongue over his lips while holding her gaze with his. "I could indeed provide my own nourishment. You'd enjoy it." His voice was soft, and silky, and terribly inviting.

There were weapons nearby, but she couldn't reach for one. She could barely breathe as heat rose through her, and she wanted desperately to go to him. He was so—compelling.

Then Wolf laughed, breaking the dark spell. He gestured toward her equipment. "Just a little revenge for being zapped. That thing gave me nightmares. Woman, you do *not* want a vampire having nightmares."

"That would be a bad idea," she agreed. What kind of nightmares did monsters have? No, she didn't want to know.

She scurried off to get dressed when he went into the kitchen.

This is a good setup, Laurent thought while he watched the cup of blood slowly spin around through the microwave's window. *Sweet.*

She's sweet—in a "thinks she's tough enough to handle me" sort of way. She looked hot and sexy when I called to her. Her expression went soft, but her eyes were hot, needy. I shouldn't have stopped. I could have made us both happy right there on the floor.

But Sid Wolf wouldn't seduce his human partner. Laurent figured it was his strong sense of self-preservation that had stopped his impulse; that wasn't the Clan way. And her believing he was a member of a Clan had its uses.

Besides, it's only a matter of time until the pretty lady succumbs to my charms. I'll have her, and she'll think it's on her terms . . . until it's too late.

"Bwaahahahaaa," he muttered.

Meanwhile, there's free meals and a place to rest. And this zapper thing to keep the bad guys at bay?

No, he didn't like that thought.

He also didn't know why having sex with Eden Faveau held any importance for him—but it did. Weird. He was having some sort of delusional fantasy about mastering a specific mortal female. Was he suicidal?

She was hunter born and bred. Better to hire her as a bodyguard than try to make her into a pet. Okay, maybe the challenge of making her need him intrigued him, because of her ancestry. But hunter women didn't even go with noble Clan boys, let alone a proudly scumbag misfit Tribe exile.

Of course, the point of mastering a woman wasn't about winning her over. Primes took. Primes possessed.

And he wanted to possess her. Oh, yeah, he really did.

Probably just because of that stupid dream.

The microwave timer beeped and Laurent took a sniff before opening the door. The animal blood in the mug was warm enough to simulate freshness, so he drank it down quickly and had the mug washed before the mortal came out of her bedroom.

He could hear her dressing, was aware of the delicious sound of cloth sliding over skin, but he didn't give in to the urge to offer to help her take it off, rather than put it on.

He really liked her scent. He remembered the texture of her lips, and the hot taste of her mouth.

He gingerly touched the fangs suddenly pressing against his lower lip. Maybe what he needed was another cup of blood to tone down the physical cravings. He was a tad on the malnourished side, what with the fighting and the running at the Patron's place. And, oh, yeah, the torture.

The mortals had bound him with silver and drugged him, all in the name of science—which was a buzz term for humans wanting to steal what nature had given to another species. Typical human behavior. They took and used and dominated—and murdered every other predator species on the planet. They were very good at justifying it, in the names of gods, in the names of progress, manifest destiny, survival of the fittest. Good versus evil, as defined by them.

"Truth, justice, and the *Homo sapiens* way."

"I thought you were a Marvel man," Faveau said, coming up behind him. "But you were paraphrasing a Superman line."

Why hadn't he noticed her arrival? It wasn't like him to be sloppy.

And why, oh why, did he find her knowing the difference between D.C. and Marvel comic-book characters so appealing, when millions of people knew the differences? He didn't find your average comic-book geek—

"Just quoting an old vampire saying," he answered.

"Really?"

"Oh, yeah. We Clan boys have a grudging

admiration for you human types. *Homo sapiens* are more than just our favorite snack."

She obviously wasn't sure if he was joking. "I see."

He'd reached into the refrigerator for the container of animal blood and held it up. "Care for a cup?"

"I'll make coffee," she answered and sidled away, carefully not looking at him.

"Tell me about this zapper thing," he said while the coffee brewed and blood warmed.

"Why don't you put some clothes on," she countered.

"Your face is diverted from my shame?"

She covered her mouth to stifle a laugh. Then she shrugged and looked him in the face. Then lower. Then back to his face. "I don't think you have anything to be ashamed of."

He grinned as he shook his head. "You're giving off some pretty mixed signals, Faveau."

"And you're not?"

"Agreed."

They turned away from each other, and lapsed into awkward silence. When the blood was ready, he carried it into the bedroom to go dress.

Chapter Six

When he came back, she was seated at the computer desk, sipping coffee. He fetched a mug of it for himself and took a seat beside her.

She was checking e-mail, and he hoped that one of the messages wasn't from a vampire named Sid Wolf, explaining why he hadn't shown up at the appointed time and place the night before.

"Anything from Clan Wolf?" he asked, prepared to run if the answer was yes.

She gave him an odd look. "Why would there be, when we're only supposed to use land lines to communicate with your people?"

"Right. Forgot the security rules for this op, what with the headache you gave me. But it's not as if the Tribes are exactly high-tech."

"They're high-tech enough to develop Dawn."

He laughed. "No way."

"Really? Do you know something I don't?"

There was nothing suspicious about her question. What he felt from her was eager curiosity. She kind of sparkled, like champagne. There was an alluring brightness to her eyes, and the way she unconsciously leaned closer to him.

Self-preservation kicked in before he did anything stupid.

"I have some suspicions," he answered.

"Like what?"

He held up a hand. "I asked you first."

Her brows came down over those bright eyes. "What question was that?"

"About this zapper device. I'm worried about it," he added with all the serious demeanor of a Clan boy he could muster. "I understand that you have it for defensive purposes, but I'd like to know what it is and how it works."

Her hunter paranoia was returning. "So you can figure out how to counter it?"

"Of course not. I like the idea of a shield that keeps vampires at bay. What I don't like is how it made me feel. I felt more like I was under psychic attack than being protected."

"It wasn't designed as a weapon," she protested.

"Of course not," he said. "Your people and mine have never been at war with each other."

She ignored this sarcasm. "Just how did it make you feel? I mean, it gave you nightmares and a headache. How bad can that be?"

He decided on honesty. "Enough so that I might have attacked you while trapped inside a nightmare. I could have hurt you without meaning to. If I hurt someone, I want to know exactly why I'm doing it. My nature is violent, and it's my job to control it. You could have turned me into a weapon. Unintentionally, of course."

She'd gone pale, and Laurent took that as a good sign.

She pointed to a device sitting on a nearby shelf. The small components looked like random stereo equipment that had met and mated during a hurricane.

"I have no idea how it works," she told him. "It's a modern addition to warding a safe house with the traditional stuff like garlic and hawthorn. It's supposed to keep vampire telepaths from finding us, not hurt anybody. I've no idea how to tone it down. My brother's the electrical engineer; I'm the software engineer side of the family."

This information caught Laurent by delighted surprise. "Really? You're a computer geek?" He desperately needed someone to break into the Patron's laptop. "You're into software?"

Eden nodded. "A girl's got to have a day job.

Nobody hunts vampires for a living these days. Do you have a day—night—job?"

"I'm a gigolo."

"Right."

"You don't believe me?"

She shook her head.

Laurent knew that if there was one thing people found irresistible, it was being asked what they did for a living in a genuinely interested tone. "What *do* you do with computers, exactly? Web design? Game development?"

"Systems security," she answered, with a proud lift of her head. Then she launched into technical terminology that left him totally lost. But he kept an interested expression on his face and went for another cup of coffee as soon as she paused for breath.

"We really ought to get to work," she said when he returned.

"The night is still very young. You don't look very well rested." He grinned. "Maybe we should go back to bed." When she looked annoyed, he added, "Or there's Hell on Earth Week on the History Channel. We wouldn't want to miss the show on Devil's Isla—"

"I've already set a tape."

"Well, then." He rubbed his hands together. "I suppose we should get to work soon."

She glanced at the computer screen. "I wish we had an update on what's been learned during the day."

His original plan had been to hang around a while longer, seduce Eden, then continue his quest to find a hacker. And maybe a Dawn dealer. He wouldn't mind giving this Dawn stuff a shot; it'd be nice to see daylight without worrying about getting a fatal sunburn. He'd had a small hope of using this zapper thing as a personal anti-vampire shield, if it could be turned down. Then she'd told him about her job.

The Families had this belief that fate played a big role in the lives of vampires. It was thought that when your life was at a major crisis and you needed your fated bondmate most, they appeared and gave you what you needed to survive. It was a lot of mystical claptrap, especially the bondmate stuff, but the belief was based on a very high percentage of coincidences that seemed to prove the point. Of course, the Families also had an old-fashioned belief in a witchy-woman moon goddess and were only slightly less matriarchal than the whipped Clan boys.

But it looked like fate or dumb luck had intervened for good, for once in his miserable life: he'd found a hacker. He still intended seduction, of course, but without any of that bonding nonsense.

He decided to answer a question Eden had asked earlier. This time it was a fair exchange rather than a gift.

"You asked if I knew something you didn't, when I was mocking the idea of the Tribes developing Dawn. I might have some information that you specifically can help with."

"Might? Me?"

It seemed logical to continue with the world-saving Clan Prime mode. The weird thing was, he *had* been involved in the noble expedition to stop the Patron.

"I picked up some information on my last assignment. There was a mortal who called himself the Patron. He was from a hunter family, the Garrisons."

She nodded, but looked disapproving. "One of the many retired families."

"Garrison was extremely wealthy. He started by stealing from Tribe Manticore, and built a fortune from his ill-gotten gains."

"Manticores? The lowest-of-the-low, scumbag Manticores once had a fortune? Who'd they steal it from?"

"From a great many people," he acknowledged. "But the point is, Garrison stole it from them. Who's the worse scumbag?" He held up a hand. "Never mind. He used his fortune to fund longevity research. Not because he wanted to help the world, but because he wanted to live forever himself. He experimented on vampires to try to find out why we live so long. The vampires were not volunteers. And some of the scientists working for him were renegades from Clan research facilities. We got it all straightened out," he concluded vaguely. "In the cleanup operation, I've come into possession of Garrison's laptop computer, but I haven't had time to do anything with it yet."

He hadn't actually stolen it from the Patron's Colorado stronghold. The laptop had been given to the Manticores as reparation by Garrison's great-granddaughter when she found out what her evil grandpa was up to. Laurent had risked his life to get the computer for the Manticores; he just hadn't bothered to turn it over to Justinian.

Whatever he did with the computer, he had to do it soon. Not only were the remnants of Justinian's pack after him, he had to worry about the information stored on the hard drive. He didn't think the Clans would do anything to block access to whatever was stored in the laptop—say, the passwords for hidden bank accounts—since the Manticores had been promised whatever financial rewards they could extract from the information. The Clans kept their promises—they were rich enough to be able to.

But humans were another worry altogether. There might be someone in the Patron's organization with access to passwords, or at least clues on how to break in. So Laurent needed to get into the computer as quickly as possible.

And now he had his very own hacker. He smiled happily at Eden Faveau. Not only was she attractive and dangerous, she was just what he needed.

"You are all I could ever ask for." He really wished that he'd remember that Tribe Primes didn't ask, they took. So he took her hand, and added, "In a technological sense, that is."

Is that all?

Laurent heard her wistful thought loud and clear. Which surprised him, because he had no sense of her being psychic. Picking up nonpsychic peoples' thoughts was possible, even fairly easy—but doing it without any deliberate effort was unusual for him.

He could see that she immediately regretted the thought and pushed it away. It made her feel weak and stupid. He watched her resolve harden, watched her remember who he was, what she was, and what their relationship was supposed to be. Maybe not adversarial at the moment, but—

"We could turn on each other at any time," he said.

Eden was surprised at the bitterness in the vampire's tone. And she was embarrassed that he could read her so easily. Most people couldn't; she'd been told that she was hard to get a handle on. Maybe Wolf saw the simple girl that she really was. Or the anti-mind-reading techniques she'd been taught weren't worth squat.

"*Will* we turn on each other?" she asked him.

"You're worried about my self-control because I don't use the daylight drugs."

"Yeah," she admitted.

"I've spent a long lifetime controlling myself without them. I need blood, I need physical release, but I've always been in charge of how I get what I need." He gave her a sharp-toothed smile. "Sex, blood, and rock and roll makes a Prime happy."

"We're not here to be happy. I need to trust that—"

"I'm in charge," he reiterated sternly. "And that's the only promise you need from me."

She stood. "Then maybe we better go out and

make you happy. You've had the blood. You're not getting the sex—"

"So I'll have to settle for the rock and roll." He tilted an eyebrow and looked knowingly at her. "At least for tonight." He got up. "We do need to get the computer. It's likely that there will be Tribe Primes to beat up along the way." He grinned, and put a bit of fang into it. "I can hardly wait."

With a bounce in her step, Eden went to gather her equipment and car keys. She couldn't help but wonder at why she found the prospect of bashing heads side-by-side with Sid Wolf such an exciting prospect.

It was clearly way too long since she'd been on a date.

Chapter Seven

"Is that why they were attacking you last night? Because of the laptop?" Eden asked.

"That was my guess," he answered.

He was staring out the front windshield of her small car, and glancing at his lean, lovely profile distracted her for a moment.

"What's it like?" she wondered. "Being able to see in the dark?"

"I don't know. It's the only way I've ever seen. What's it like walking in the sunshine?"

"You could find that out anytime you wanted to. But I'll never see in the dark."

She cringed when she heard the wistfulness in her voice. She was prepared for some scathing comment about a vampire hunter envying a vampire, but she received a gentle smile instead.

"Curiosity is normal," he said. "At least for our kind."

"*Our kind?*"

"We're the ones who know that the world isn't what most people think it is. We know that we're different. Me, because I'm not human. You, because you know that I exist. Our knowledge shuts us off from the *real* world. All we have is each other. We can't help but be curious."

"Don't your kind want to be part of the real world? Isn't that why you developed the drugs?"

"I have no idea why the daylight drugs were developed."

"You just don't personally approve of using them?"

"I don't disapprove of those who do. Don't your people want to let us be part of the real world, so you can have normal lives, too?"

"Yes," she answered. "At least I do."

Eden hadn't meant to confide that truth to anyone, ever. The Faveaus had been doing this vampire-hunting crap *forever.* Some ancestors had taken some kind of *Da Vinci Code* secret-society vow to protect the world from evil through all their generations, and now she was stuck with it. Nobody had asked her if she wanted in on the family avocation.

She tried not to resent it, tried to think noble thoughts and do noble deeds. Defending the world was an honor and the right thing to do. Most of the time.

"I want to go to Hawaii," she said. "I want to see lava."

"But instead you're stuck hauling my pale ass around town in a VW Beetle hunting some holy grail of a computer, right?"

"Right." She glared at him. "How'd you know I was thinking of that holy grail book?"

"Lucky guess."

She doubted it. But if he wasn't reading her mind, they really *were* too much alike. Maybe he was right about their being alike, in a world view sense.

"But your people see mine as prey."

"And vice versa."

"Okay, I can see how you'd see it that way."

He laughed. "If you'd care to check our shared history, you'd find that hunters have taken out far more vampires than vampires have humans."

"What about the Kiev Massacre of 1405?"

"That was done by a crazy lone Prime with some kind of blood sickness."

"That's the cover story the Clans offered. Our records say differently."

"Well, neither of us were there, so I doubt we'll ever know the truth."

He sounded a mite testy, and she supposed she did, too. The hot button issue they were talking about certainly wasn't helpful for their business relationship, so Eden attempted to concentrate on the assignment. It didn't help that they were sitting so closely together in her small car. The proximity hinted at intimacy.

She knew that he was uncomfortable because of the strips of silver around the doors and windows and the silver censer filled with garlic hanging from the rearview mirror. The back seat was filled with her equipment. What she wasn't wearing, that is. There were also a few things tucked under her seat and in pockets on the driver's-side door.

Mind you, while the vampire was uncomfortable, he'd smiled approval when he'd gotten into the car last night—well, grimaced as he gingerly took a seat. "Better safe than sorry," he'd said.

Last night his comfort hadn't mattered to her, and maybe it shouldn't now. But—even if he wasn't her guest, he was her partner. Last night she'd thought of him only as a dangerous, not-quite-trustworthy temporary ally. Getting to know him a little made him more dangerous than ever, in ambiguous, complicated ways. Last night she'd found his proximity in the small car disturbing simply because of *what* he was.

Tonight, layered over the knowledge that she was too close to a vampire was the electric awareness of Wolf as a male. She'd been trained to ignore the potent masculinity of Primes, but the training wasn't working.

She tried to clear her mind of the awareness her body couldn't deny, and get on with the job.

"So you went up against the Manticores," she said, in an effort to both have a conversation and gather information. "Are they as nasty as I've heard? Was old Justinian involved? They're daring to show their fangs back in San Diego? Are we likely to be attacked by any sexist pig Manticores? Because I would love to stake them right through their tiny little di—"

"Turn right at the next light."

She didn't have to be psychic to be aware of how tense he'd become, and how curious.

"Is there something about the Manticores I don't know?" Eden asked.

He was silent for a minute, then he said, "Apparently there's a lot about the Manticores I don't know. Tell me about them. And no Prime's dick is that little," he added.

Eden had to bite her tongue. "Let's make this

a mutual exchange, shall we? Of information," she added hastily.

"Pull in here," he said, indicating the entrance to a mall parking lot. "Let's see if anything nasty comes looking for us."

"I haven't detected anyone following."

He tapped his forehead. "I've got a little telepathic buzz going. Might not be anything, but I'm not about to lead anyone to the laptop. The night's young enough to exercise a bit of patience and caution."

They'd already been driving in circles for over an hour. Ever-widening circles, Eden had to admit, cautiously weaving through areas with heavy traffic and quieter side streets.

"I wouldn't mind getting attacked," Eden told him, but she pulled into a parking space. She killed the engine and lights. "If we take a prisoner, you can read his mind for information about who's dealing Dawn."

"But the information on the computer might tell us who is manufacturing the drug, and where. For all we know, the Patron himself might have been selling the drug to vampires, using the money to fund his research. Shutting down the source will get the drug off the streets."

"Good plan."

"Of course," he added thoughtfully after a moment, "the drug isn't actually illegal by any mortal laws, and I haven't seen any clinical proof that it causes psychotic behavior."

"You're splitting ethical hairs." Wolf's attitude was downright disturbing. "If we capture a few Tribe users, your scientists can study them."

"Like lab rats."

"That's an insult to rats. The point of this operation is to keep monsters like the Manticores from inhabiting the world twenty-four/seven."

Wolf turned to face her. She assumed his psychic senses were on watch for any approaching vampires, while his gaze was turned intently on her.

"Ah, yes, the Manticores." His silky tone was practically a purr. He put a hand on her arm, the touch warm and electric. "Tell me all about the Manticores. From the beginning."

Eden felt almost hypnotized. Not threatened or anything, but she very much welcomed the opportunity to share a bit of knowledge. She lived in two worlds, and the secrets of her nighttime life were hard to bear. Here was someone from outside her own claustrophobic little circle but still in on it all. Someone new to talk to, someone interested in what she had to say. She and Wolf were—

"Manticores?" he prompted.

"Right. Sorry, I think the change in my sleep patterns is making me unfocused," she finished.

"And here I thought it was my overwhelmingly sensual effect on you."

"No. That's just irritating."

He put a hand on her thigh. "You're not denying it."

Eden had to concentrate hard, but she pretended his touch didn't affect her, and went on. "The hunters first encountered the Manticores in the Middle Ages, though there are some scanty ancient records preserved in monasteries in the Sinai that link a whole bunch of tribes with names that pertain to dragons to a Middle Eastern god, or demon. They worshipped this dragon god or—"

"Demon." He snorted. "Our version is that the dragon-born vampires kept this creature as a pet and used him to extort tribute from mortals. But do go on, the human version is probably much more relevant for hunting Manticores."

She hadn't heard about the pet and extortion theory, but his comment made her think that this dragon of legend might really have existed. And why not? If the world could have vampires in it, it followed that other mythical creatures also existed. Just because her family specialized in one kind of hunting didn't mean that there weren't other things to hunt.

"The night world is bigger than I've been led to believe, isn't it?"

He grinned. "Oh, the creatures I've seen and heard of. No doubt sometime in the future, we'll all have separate cable channels and equal rights advocates lobbying in Washington. But that's for the future. You're giving me a history lesson now."

"While we wait to be attacked," she added, and took a quick glance outside the car's windows. She didn't see anything, so she went on. "The one thing we've been certain of about the Manticores from the fifteenth century on, is that they specialize in slave dealing, within and outside the vampire community. Mostly they kidnap human women, but they take Family and Clan females when they can. The humans they train as sex slaves, but vampires are used as breeders."

"You make it all sound so sleazy. Manticores consider this a valuable service within their community."

She gave him a disgusted look. "I wouldn't think a Clan Prime would joke about such a thing."

"Bad taste." He shrugged. "The Clans do not

take losing their females lightly. No vampire does."

"You don't have that many women," she said. "You have to protect them for self-preservation, even more than the duty, honor, and respect you claim toward your matriarchs."

"We do need to keep the species going."

"The children you have with mortal women don't inherit many vampire traits. I've heard that they're called mules by vampires."

He lifted his head proudly. "No Clan Prime would ever call his child by such a derogatory name. I've heard that hunters call such children abominations."

Okay, she'd baited him, he'd baited back. She let it go. "A pack or two of Manticores came to America in the early 1800s. They settled in the Five Points area of New York City, where they fed and preyed on the poverty-stricken immigrant community. Then the Family Caeg moved in and drove them out of New York. They moved south to New Orleans, and out to the Californian gold fields. Wherever they went, people disappeared, especially young women. In the wilder parts of the country, those women were openly used as prostitutes. By the end of the century they operated brothels in several California cities, as well as dealing slaves to other tribes. Over several months at the turn of the twentieth century, the hunters burned down the Manticores' brothels and freed the women."

"Didn't the newspapers of the time report all this as some sort of gang warfare? Criminal elements at war with each other? And they editorialized about how both sides needed to be stopped," he said.

"And weren't some of the newspapers of the time owned by Clan members?"

"That I know nothing about. Really. Go on; tell me all about *old* Justinian."

He had that seductive tone again, as if he was urging her on to some sin. Eden wondered if that was a Prime thing, or if it was just him. And his hand was still on her thigh. She was exquisitely *aware* of his touch, of his presence. She had to take a deep, steadying breath, but at least that didn't draw a smug chuckle from him. She began to suspect that he wasn't noticing being hot.

"Justinian *is* old," she finally went on. "We have reports about him killing and raping going back at least three hundred years. He has a lot of followers, even though he's never been officially the king Prime of the tribe. His exploits have made him popular among his peers."

"Oh, yeah? Like what?"

The Clan vampire's almost admiring tone confused her. "You guys claim to loathe the likes of Justinian."

"We give points for style."

"He's a slimy, slippery, altogether putrid excuse for a semi-sentient living being. He ran the Manticore sex slave operation. He breaks women and turns them out. He's been a pimp for centuries."

"Is that how he built up the fortune stolen by Garrison?"

"It would have to be. You do know that he started a war between the Manticores and local clans, including yours, back in the 1880s? In fact, it was over his stealing a female from the Wolf Clan, wasn't it? We hunters don't know many of the details, even though we helped run the tribes out of town. Did you ever get her back?"

He had gone very still. He was staring out the windshield, his expression blank. "No."

For all that his answer was brusque and cold, it made her aware that in some way he was hurting and vulnerable. It occurred to Eden that Sid Wolf was likely related to the kidnapped Wolf female. What was somebody else's ancient history for her might be a recent tragedy for the long-lived Clan.

"Did you know her?"

He gave her a look that made her wish she'd kept her mouth shut.

"Do you know that you're hurting me?" she asked.

Chapter Eight

Laurent hadn't realized his claws were out. Or that he had such a tight grip on the mortal's leg. He wished he could get some pleasure from hurting her, but it didn't ease his own pain at all. So he let her go.

He even said, "Sorry."

Her words echoed around in his head.

Did you ever get her back?

"I never saw her again."

"What?"

Laurent realized that he must have spoken aloud, because the woman beside him was no telepath. She did have a talent, though. She was cursed with the ability to make him remember things he'd deliberately buried—things best *left* buried.

Not that he wasn't to blame as well. He'd

been the one who'd given in to sudden curiosity about his sire. His *possible* sire. Justinian had teased him about the connection all the years Laurent spent under the pack leader's thumb. Laurent had even let the old bastard use the promise of truth at last to get under his skin again a few weeks ago. It was one of the reasons he'd gone along with the scheme to retrieve the Manticore fortune from the Patron.

Justinian used knowledge as punishment, reward, and torture. Laurent had seen Justinian break the women he trained with words as much as with beatings. The pack leader wasn't any kinder to the vampires he ruled.

Laurent fell for it, briefly. Then he learned that Justinian wanted revenge against the Garrison family even more than he wanted the money, while Laurent was strictly in it for the money.

Laurent shook his head. He had to get away from the pack. He had to get on with his life. Nostalgia was stupid. Curiosity was stupid. How had he allowed himself to be so self-indulgent?

"Are you all right?"

Her hand was on his shoulder. It was warm—and comforting.

He pushed it away as though it burned.

He didn't need a human's touch for anything but pleasure. Justinian was right—break them, use them, make them pay for their life in the light, and—!

Then Laurent calmed down as he suddenly recalled that he *was* using Eden. She was his ticket to all the wealth he'd ever dreamed of.

"I don't mean to be scary," he murmured in his most soothing tone.

She eyed him warily. He suspected she was holding a weapon in the hand he couldn't see, and he didn't blame her. "What's the matter with you?" she demanded.

He told her the truth, all the while reveling in the irony of how the truth could be twisted. "Hearing about Justinian's past had a strong effect on me."

"Gave you a longing to rescue all those maidens in distress, did it?"

He heard the longing that the Clan boy beside her really was a hero, and it twisted something inside him. He reminded himself that he did not come equipped with a conscience.

"It's too late to save anyone," he told her.

Then his attention was drawn back to the outside world. He smiled.

"Something wicked this way comes?" she asked, alert to his reaction.

He nodded. "And just when I'm in the mood to do some damage."

She was suddenly hyper alert, and all business. "How many? Where are they coming from."

He reluctantly admired this side of the mortal, even though it was no way for a female to behave. "Modern women," he murmured.

"Don't know our place," she added for him.

"I could rise to the bait and say something sexist and sexually provocative here."

"But we don't have the time." She started the car and eased out of the parking space.

He stroked her bruised thigh. "Remind me to kiss this and make it all better. Where are we going?"

She turned toward the nearest exit. "We don't want a riot at the mall."

"No witnesses or collateral damage," he agreed.

"Do you think they'll notice that we've been waiting for them to ambush us?"

He chuckled. "Tribe boys? They have the same instincts as a greyhound—they see a rabbit and they run after it. In this case, a bug," he said, patting the dashboard.

"A tricked-out bug," she answered. "Don't let her staid outer appearance fool you."

Laurent looked the mortal woman over with growing hunger. "Oh, I won't," he told her.

He felt the heat of her blush across the short distance between them, but resisted the impulse to stroke warm, soft skin. Her attraction to him was further balm to his frayed nerves, and he was going to make very good use of that attraction.

Then he focused on their opponents. He let his shielding down for a moment, sending a bolt of surprise and fear, as though he had just discovered them. He'd felt a trio of them circling the perimeter of the huge parking lot; they'd been faintly aware of the mental scent he'd been broadcasting at a very low level. When he lowered his shielding he picked up more information, as well as broadcasting it.

"A pair of Manticore," he said. "And a Hydra, I think. The Hydra is hunting alone." He pondered the meaning of this. "Two for me, one for you, maybe."

"What makes you think that?"

"My guess is that the Hydra is involved with the drug dealers. It's likely that the dealers want the human hunters to leave them alone. He probably intends to make an example out of you."

"Interesting," Eden said. "So if they aren't together, can we use that against them?"

"Get them to mix it up with each other? Turn

it into a hunting dispute?" That would make an excellent diversion to get the Manticores off his tail long enough to get the computer. "I like your thinking, girl."

She gave him a disgusted look, but otherwise let the *girl* go. "We can take them out while they're fighting each other."

He nodded, though fighting the others was not part of the plan he intended to carry out. "Good strategy. They're all after us now. Let's find a place were we can bring them together."

"Stay in the car."

"I'm not staying in the car," Eden answered. "Stop being chivalrous."

"I'm not being chivalrous. I want you to keep the engine running while I get the Manticores to chase me."

The night before, it had all happened so fast that she'd gotten through the action without thinking about it. Years of training fueled by adrenaline took her through the attack on the vampires. Now, with weapons and an ally by her side, she was nervous about the whole thing. She wasn't sure if bickering with Wolf was helping her nerves, or making them worse.

His high-handed *We'll do this, this, and this* wasn't helping.

"I am not just your wheelman," she told him. "If they're after both of us, we should both show ourselves."

"You can't run fast enough."

She knew that the Manticore Primes were following them in a van as she drove sedately along an empty street lined with warehouses. They'd been playing hide-and-seek on the city streets with this pair for some time now, trying to make the vampires think that they were attempting to elude them.

Wolf claimed to have a headache from the mental threats the others were tossing his way. He also claimed the Hydra was nearby, watching the chase and getting more and more annoyed with the Manticore interference in his hunt.

"This is such a waste of the night." Wolf slapped the dashboard. "Don't these idiots know I'm on a tight schedule?"

Eden glared at him. "You've got hundreds of years. I'm the one giving up my vacation for this."

He glared back. "Right, you want to go see volcanos. Why? Do you have a magic ring you need to get rid of?"

Eden laughed. And realized that perhaps the vampire was running on nerves as much as she was. Or maybe it was all adrenaline and blood lust in his case.

"The last time I saw lava, I was running from it. I don't like running from things," she told him.

"Runnin—"

"Let's do this," she said, and braked, spun, and gunned the little car toward the large van.

"This is *not* the plan!" Wolf shouted as the van swerved out of the Volkswagen's way.

The van scraped the side of a building and came to a halt. Eden spun her car in another tight turn and came to a stop. The Manticores were already out of the van and running toward them.

"Go!" she called to Wolf.

He was out of the car instantly. The trio of vampires met in the street, full in the glare of the VW's headlights.

Eden moved quickly, but armed herself before setting off toward the fight. She stayed in the shadows. And she watched the shadows. The vampires moved in a swift, silent dance. And the shadow that came out of the shadows moved with equal speed and silence. Eden saw the Hydra Prime because she was concentrating all her attention on finding him. The moment she was certain that the moving darkness was her quarry, she fired a crossbow bolt at him.

The short arrow was made of hawthorn, tipped with silver, and treated with a garlic-based coating. Any of the three ingredients would stop a vampire, but this centuries-tested combination had saved many a mortal hunter's life. She'd killed a vampire with such an arrow last night. Right now her intention was to wound.

The arrow hit the vampire in the shoulder. He yowled in pain, but that didn't stop him turning and running toward her. This didn't give her time to aim carefully as she shot the vampire again. The second hit was in the thigh, and this time he went down.

"And stay there!" Eden called as she ran past the downed vampire to help Wolf.

"Get back!" Laurent shouted as he noticed Eden's approach out of the corner of his eye.

Worry jolted through him, taking him totally by surprise, fueling his anger at the Primes he was fighting. He didn't need help. He didn't want her help. A girl could get hurt in this kind of brawl.

A fist jammed into his jaw.

He could get hurt in this kind of brawl!

He swore, and kicked his attacker in the chest.

As the first Prime flew backward, the second came up behind Laurent.

"Traitor!"

Why did they always feel the need to talk? The trouble with vampires was that they were always into melodrama—and it wasn't just his fellow tribesmen. Only the Family members seemed to make any effort at just getting on with a normal life.

"Why couldn't I have been born into a Family?" he muttered, and turned to knock the first vampire down again.

It dodged around him.

The second one came up behind him again, and whispered in Laurent's ear. "He offers an exchange of property."

"Justinian has nothing I want."

"He says you will—once you think about the cravings you share."

"This is a fight, not a negotiation," Laurent answered.

The first Manticore was moving toward Eden, and the second joined him.

She was kneeling in the middle of the street, taking aim with her crossbow. She couldn't take both of them with her medieval weapon;

one of them was going to rip her throat out.

"That's *my* human!" he shouted, and rushed to her defense.

Things happened too damn fast with vampires! She'd been well trained, but seeing the triple blur of deadly speed coming toward her was almost panic-inducing. She held her ground and fired an arrow.

Her target dodged easily, then they were on her.

She managed to spray concentrated garlic juice into the face of one of them.

While he dropped to the ground screaming, the second one grabbed her by the upper arms. She caught a glimpse of fangs and glowing eyes, then claws bit deep into her flesh and muscles, and there was horrible pain. The thing lifted her to her feet and the fanged mouth bent toward her throat . . .

Then the third blur was upon them.

Knocked to the ground, Eden clutched at her bleeding arms while a battle swirled at light speed around her. A body fell heavily beside her. The head followed a moment later.

Everything went black for a while, after that.

The next thing Eden knew, Wolf said, "Drink this, it'll help."

She took a sip of warm liquid that sent energizing lightning through her, then a hungry gulp. At first she thought it was hundred-proof moonshine. Then she realized she was drinking vampire blood—and all she wanted was more.

Chapter Nine

"That's enough." Laurent gently eased Eden's head away from his bleeding wrist. She shuddered and moaned in a way that excited the hell out of him, but he was firm. "Save some for me."

He wasn't in the habit of sharing his blood with anyone, but she'd been bleeding profusely, and his reaction had been automatic. It was pure self-preservation, that's all—she was his ticket to a better life.

He rose and helped her to her feet, noticing that the one she'd stunned had gotten away. He turned Eden away from the remains of the one he'd killed, but he gave a quick glance over his shoulder.

He hadn't realized he'd used so much force. But the impulse to save Eden had been so strong . . .

He didn't get it.

"We have to get out of here," he told her, glancing up at the sky. Somewhere along the way he'd lost track of time. He was feeling light-headed, both from the loss of blood and from the pleasure that came with it. Giving was as much a rush as getting, and he was hard from it.

"What was that for?" she asked, sounding wasted and ragged.

She leaned heavily against him, and he was tempted to pick her up and carry her. But once she recovered from the orgasms, she'd realize she was fully healed—maybe even strong enough to carry him.

"Medicinal purposes, to stop your bleeding. It worked," he added.

"You okay?" she asked.

"Horny."

She nodded. "Right. That's one of the effects vampires experience when they share blood with mortals."

He smiled at her lecturing tone. "We didn't share. That—wouldn't be polite behavior for a Clan boy." He wanted to taste her, though. The scent of her blood gave him a hint of what her taste would be like.

He deliberately stepped away from her.

She wobbled a bit, but then deliberately stood

straight and squared her shoulders. "Thank you," she said, giving him a formal nod.

He crossed his arms to keep from grabbing her—then he grabbed her anyway. And kissed her.

This time her arms slid around him, her body molded to his, and she kissed him back. Heat seared between them.

Her eagerness and the intensity of his own need stunned him. He wanted *her*—body, blood, and soul.

If Laurent hadn't taught himself to keep control of his instincts, he would have had her then and there. Fighting back the rising hunger for Eden was the hardest thing he'd ever done.

Needing anyone is the most dangerous trap in the world.

Laurent held Eden away by her shoulders. "We better get out of here."

It took her a moment to catch her breath and gather her wits. "We've turned the place into a crime scene," she acknowledged. "I can get my people in to clean it up." She glanced to her left. "But we can't leave just yet."

Laurent looked at the sky. "You do remember that I don't work days."

"I know." She took his hand and tugged him toward the van that was skewed across the sidewalk.

"And what happened to our original plan— partner? Weren't we supposed to let them fight each other while we went for the computer?" He could scent the third vampire's blood now and found this disturbing. "What did you do?"

"I wounded one." She paused for a moment and looked at Laurent contritely. "I'm sorry I acted on impulse. Your plan was a good one, but I saw a chance to get needed information and had to act on it."

She led him around the van, and he saw the wounded vampire lying between the van and the warehouse wall.

"You need to interrogate him." Eden stepped back and made a call on her cell phone while Laurent stared between her and the bleeding Hydra Prime.

"*I* need to . . . ?"

Then Laurent saw it from her point of view. The Hydra had come after her with intent to kill. To her, the bad guy was a dealer in a drug the humans considered dangerous. Besides, the minute the arrows were taken out, the Hydra would start to heal—and would likely try to attack Eden again. This war between mortals and Tribes had been going on for a long time, and neither side saw the other as sentient beings.

Laurent didn't know why he had any sympathy for mortals himself, but he always had. Maybe because he'd been hunted by vampires himself. He could never completely be on the humans' side, but face it, Tribe vampires *needed* the ruthlessness of the hunters to keep their savage behavior in check. His whole species would have gotten itself destroyed by humans long ago if the reckless Tribes weren't kept in check.

Eden was one tough chick: she did what she had to to get the job done. He shouldn't admire her for that. Deadly, free-thinking women were *not* attractive. In fact, he'd recently given a Prime from Clan Reynard that advice about his dangerous bondmate—not that the Reynard had listened. It bothered Laurent that he was beginning to see why Colin Foxe had found his Mia so sexy.

There was a certain edgy sexiness to Eden that made her incredibly hot to him. Making love to her would be risky business. The thought of it made his blood sing.

Of course, the downside was that if she actually knew who he was, she'd turn all her deadly skills on him.

Of course, dealing with that would be kind of fun, too.

Laurent shook his head.

"Well?" Eden said, stepping up beside him.

He slid his arm around her waist and drew her close without a second thought. "Well, what?"

"Have you found out anything?"

"What I know is that dawn isn't far away. Are your people coming?"

"On the way."

"Then we need to get going."

"You're a telepath," she reminded him. "Have you talked to him?"

Laurent was outraged. "That's invasion of privacy! Vampires don't do that to each other!"

"You do it to humans."

"That's different. It's for humans' own good," he added, trying to remember his role.

This brought a snort of derision. "Are you Clan people really as noble as your PR claims? We're in a hurry. All you have to do is read his surface thoughts. Make him tell us what he knows about Dawn, then we'll let him go."

"I'm lying right here," the Hydra rasped. "Ask me anything."

"I want truth," Eden said.

"Get these sticks out of me," the Hydra said to Laurent. "The silver burns."

Laurent didn't know why he was reluctant to probe the other vampire's thoughts. The Hydra was weak, helpless to defend himself.

Justinian would have ripped open an enemy vampire's mind without any compunction; Laurent had watched him do it. He'd felt the madness descend on Justinian's victim as well. He'd been told he was weak for feeling sorry for the victims, and it was true. Pity was weakness. Compassion was weakness.

Indifference—now, that was an acceptable survival trait. He managed indifference quite well most of the time.

The Hydra was staring at him, his expression full of pain, but also calculation.

"What?" Laurent asked.

"Don't I know you?"

He recognized the other vampire now; a scumbag with the unfortunate name of Roswald. They weren't well acquainted, but they had worked a couple of smuggling operations together many decades ago.

Laurent stepped quickly away from Eden.

"You're no—" Roswald began as Laurent knelt beside him.

Laurent put his hand over the vampire's mouth. "Silence." He leaned close and whispered in the Hydra's ear. "Rat me out, and you're dead."

He stared into the other vampire's eyes while the earth rolled inexorably toward sunrise. It seemed to take hours before the other vampire acknowledged Laurent's dominance by looking away.

How you doing, Wally? Laurent asked, entering the other's mind.

The Hydra offered no resistance. *Been better. What are you doing with the monkey bitch?*

Working a scam.

Ah. I see. This really hurts.

You taking this Dawn drug? Or is the sun going to wreck your complexion in a few minutes?

The jolt of fear that went through Roswald told Laurent that the other vampire wasn't a user.

Are you a dealer, then? A smart dealer doesn't use his own product.

It doesn't work that way, Wally answered. *You know the drill with our kind.*

"Sounds like somebody hasn't given him permission to use Dawn," Laurent told Eden.

It was hard to communicate verbally while he was touching another mind, but Eden was anxiously waiting for information.

"How does he get permission?" she asked.

"By killing the hunter that's after his boss," Laurent answered. *Right?* he asked Roswald.

"Right," Roswald answered aloud.

"Who is your boss?" Eden asked the prisoner. "Where do we find him?"

Can I lie to her? Roswald asked Laurent.

Fine with me.

Even as Laurent answered the verbal thought, he slipped deeper into the other vampire's mind. He found out the truth about who was in charge of the drug dealing, and other pertinent details. Maybe he did it for the challenge, maybe he did it because the information might prove valuable to him.

He suspected he did it because Eden wanted him to.

Which was not a good reason at all. Playing into the hands of the good guys was not profitable. Or safe. Or sane.

The safe and sane thing would be to keep the knowledge to himself as a card to play, when and if he needed it for his own sake.

Remember that, he told himself, and stepped away from Roswald.

"You can let him go now," he told Eden.

"But—"

"I said you would if he talked. You did hurt him."

"He was trying to kill me!"

"He promised not to try again. Sure, he's a Dawn dealer, and he's a Tribe boy, but he deserves some reparations for pain and torture." Laurent hoped he sounded enough like a stern and compassionate member of the Wolf Clan to get through to her.

He glanced toward the east, where the sky was turning the faintest shade of pink. Damn. The night was gone, and he was no closer to acquiring vast amounts of wealth than he had been twenty-four hours before.

Which meant he was going to have to spend another day as Sid Wolf, the brave and noble. . . .

He shuddered at the thought.

"Okay, okay, we'll let him go."

He smiled as his partner knelt on the sidewalk and carefully eased the hawthorn and silver arrows out of Roswald. She didn't look so tough now. She was all wincing tenderness as she eased the pain she'd caused.

"You're a bundle of contradictions, Faveau," Laurent told her. "First you hurt 'em, then you heal 'em."

She gave him a quick glance. "I'm just trying to figure out how to do this job. There," she said as she finished taking the second arrow out.

She sat back on her heels, and Laurent made sure to get between her and the Hydra as Roswald staggered to his feet.

The other vampire gave him a venomous

look, but he was weak, and it was too near sunrise for him to cause any trouble. Roswald limped hurriedly away, his form caught briefly in the headlights of a van as it turned into the street.

"Your people are here," Laurent said.

He felt his skin begin to warm, even though the sun hadn't topped the horizon yet. The uncomfortable sensation emphasized the appeal of daylight drugs, whether they were sanctioned or the street variety.

He urged Eden toward her Volkswagen. "Report later," he told her. "I have to get out of here."

Chapter Ten

"You have a sunburn. How can you have a sunburn from a few seconds exposure?"

Eden heard the whining complaint in her voice, but the truth was, she was feeling guilty for being the cause of exposing Wolf to the sunlight. The street had been completely empty, so she shouldn't have stopped at the red light on the corner in front of the apartment building. By the time she turned into the underground garage, Wolf was blistered.

"I'm sorry," she said as she pulled into a parking space.

He'd been silent the whole drive, but she'd been aware of the tension building in him with the growing daylight. Now that they were inside the garage, he heaved a sigh and touched her arm.

"Don't worry about it. I heal fast." He got

out of the car, then opened her door for her in a very polite, old-fashioned way.

Eden smiled at this chivalrous gesture. He smiled back. It sent a hot shiver through her, even though the smile didn't completely reach his eyes. And the sexy edge of danger he exuded made her knees weak.

His blood sang in her. Sang, and sent hot desire curling all through her.

"You're still mad at me about something, aren't you?" she managed as they walked toward the elevator. Even though she was going up in flames, she told herself the desire would wear off, and that they still had to work together.

"Not angry. Frustrated." He took her hand as they stepped into the elevator. "And not really at you." He yawned. "And not really sleepy, either. Just—" He shrugged. "I want to get on with my life."

"Yeah, me too," she agreed. "But we have to stop the Dawn dealers first."

He shrugged again, and silence stretched between them as the elevator crept upward. Eden was all too aware of the warmth of his skin, and the latent strength of the hand holding hers. Wolf leaned against the rear wall of the car, staring straight ahead. He looked very pale in the

harsh overhead light, and the dark circles under
his eyes emphasized the sharp outline of his
cheekbones. At least his sunburn had already
healed.

"You don't look good," she ventured. The
truth was, despite the evidence of exhaustion, he
was still the handsomest male she'd ever seen.

"Montserrat" was his answer.

"What?"

"What about Stromboli?"

"Huh?"

"Or there's Mount Etna. Iceland has an active
geological life you could check out."

Eden finally realized that everywhere he'd
mentioned was the site of lava flows. "I doubt
they allow tourists on Monserrat," she told him.
"The island is still one big erupting volcano."

"You said the last time you saw lava, you
were running from it. What's that about?"

"When I was a kid, my family went on vacation in the Andes. The village where we stayed
was at the base of a dormant volcano."

He nodded. "It wasn't dormant when you
left."

"When we ran for our lives," she said. "We
were on the last truck out during the evacua-
tion. I remember looking back as the lava
burned down the mountain. I saw it torch the

first house on the outskirts of the village, and the fire leaping from building to building. It was inexorable. Terrifying." She sighed. "Beautiful."

"So you want to see it again."

"Yes. I figure looking at lava in Hawaii is safer than my initial experience."

"You're a vampire hunter." He grinned at her. "What do you know about being safe?"

"I'm not suicidal."

"Having adventures isn't about being safe. Life isn't about being safe."

"I know that."

"Do you?" His voice was a soft, sultry purr.

Suddenly she didn't think he was talking about volcanoes anymore. The dangerous fire was in his eyes, and Eden couldn't look away. She'd always been drawn to fire.

She wasn't sure what would have happened next, but the elevator stopped, and they stepped away from each other as a man got on.

The rest of the ride up to the fifth floor was uneventful. Desire wasn't racing through her anymore as they reached the apartment, but it was a slow, persistent ache.

She ached in other ways as well. His blood had healed the deep cuts on her arms, and she'd regained her energy, but she wasn't yet used to living by night.

"I hope this case doesn't go on too much longer," she said as she stepped into the living room. "Because the hours are killing me."

"It might not just be the hours, if this goes on much longer."

A chill went down her spine at the coldness in his voice, but she faced the danger. "Having a personal vendetta against me is—a challenge."

He went into the galley kitchen and took a container of blood from the refrigerator. Her immediate temptation was to offer herself instead, but she knew that was the way bonds were formed. He'd only been trying to help her when he'd given her his blood. The fact that he didn't now assume she was there for his sustenance was a good sign of his honorable intentions. Her resentment of those honorable intentions was only a by-product of what had happened.

"I'm going to take a shower," she said, and left him to his meal.

By the time she was done, Wolf had retreated to his bedroom. She needed to sleep, too, but there were a few things to take care of before she could rest.

The phone rang before she could even sit down at the desk to check her e-mail.

"Yes? What? Where? No, he can't come out in the daylight. But I'll be right there."

Eden put down the phone and ran her hands through her damp hair. No rest for the wicked, she supposed, glaring at Wolf's closed door before hurrying to dress.

There was a hint of vampire on the morning breeze. Joe took note of it, but didn't think much about it. He'd spent a long night on a stakeout where absolutely nothing had happened. And on his night off, too, all alone, which increased the sense of aggravation he'd been nursing lately.

It really made him want to bite something.

Right now, all he wanted was to watch waves rolling onto the beach and sip his tall paper cup of black coffee out here on the café patio. He liked the smell of the sea. He liked watching the girls go by.

He liked—

He took a deep breath. Something wasn't right. The nose knew.

The nose knew the scent of fear, and the reek of aggression. It was on the breeze, coming from the same direction as the scent of vampires.

He didn't immediately equate the vampires with the other scents. The one vampire he knew was Clan, who would consider it rude to go around scaring mortals in public.

Joe didn't really want to get involved, but curiosity was strong in him. So was the need to help. It seemed almost instinctual, which made him feel kind of domesticated, which he hated.

Still, if there were a couple of vampires inadvertently outing themselves with bad behavior, it behooved a member of another supernatural species to look into the situation. After all, if people found out about vampires, how long would it be before suspicions of the existence of werefolk were voiced in anything but the tabloids?

Joe took his coffee with him as he headed up the street toward the source of trouble. People strolling in the Sunday-morning crowd didn't consciously notice the speed and suppleness with which he moved around them, but they did get out of his way.

It didn't take him long to reach the entrance of a café courtyard where little tables were set around a blue-and-yellow-tiled fountain. It was very like the patio of the coffee shop he'd left.

Only here, some of the tables were turned over, and there was a dead dove in the fountain, its blood staining the water. A vampire stood at the top of the fountain. Though no fangs were showing, he was plucking startled birds from the air at lightning speed, draining them and tossing them aside.

The other vampire was quietly and methodically building a sculpture out of all the metal furniture in the courtyard. He was constructing a tower, and making no secret of his preternatural strength as he bent and twisted chairs and tables into the shapes he wanted.

Both vampires frequently paused to look into the bright blue sky.

Are they waiting to be struck by lightning? Joe wondered. Or sunstroke?

"They've been acting odd for a while," he heard someone say. "But the cops I called are just standing there and watching them. One of them made a phone call, but no one's done anything."

"Maybe it's not against the law to kill pigeons?" someone else said.

"But it's scaring away customers and drawing a crowd at the same time."

"Do something," a woman urged the officers, who stood motionless by one of the tall flowering bushes at the courtyard entrance.

Joe got the distinct impression that the two cops were waiting for someone else to come and fix the problem for them. Maybe they'd called for backup.

Maybe they knew what they were facing, and

were waiting for supernatural backup. Joe knew very well that this was a crazy thought, but he didn't think it was wrong. The thing was—he wasn't sure if there was anything he could or should do.

Then the vampire in the fountain focused his attention on a young woman in the crowd. He snarled and jumped to the ground, and Joe had no choice but to act.

The woman turned and ran, headed toward the beach. Joe sped into the men's room of the coffee shop to get naked and change into a one-hundred-and-sixty-pound black wolf. He propped the door open with a shoe before he took animal form, then nosed it the rest of the way open.

In this form it was even easier for him to follow the scent of sick vampires.

"Report!" Eden shouted to the cops as she finally made it through the crowd heading in the opposite direction. She joined the officers in running toward the water. Besides being on the police force, the pair were also her cousins Charlie and Andre, and vampire hunters.

"Both subjects took off. One of them away from the scene. The other—"

"You're not tracking him?"

"The other one is chasing a woman."

"Okay."

Saving a civilian was definitely more important than tracking a lone vampire right now.

"Pick up his trail after this is over," she directed.

They were within sight of the water now. The brine scent filled her lungs. People on the crowded walkway saw the cops and got out of the way. What she didn't expect was to have someone come up behind her and push her aside.

What was even more surprising was that it wasn't a person that passed her, but an enormous black dog. She and her partners ended up following the animal out onto the sand. It led the way toward the vampire.

It said a lot about the vampire's weakened physical state that he hadn't caught up to the fleeing woman yet. The dog made a great leap, and landed square and hard on the vampire's back. Normally this wouldn't have done any good, despite the animal's great size and the force of the hit. A normal Prime would have simply shaken the dog off.

This Prime went down face-first on the beach, and didn't move as the animal's powerful jaws wrapped around the back of his neck.

This had to be a trained police dog, Eden decided. It lifted its head as they reached the prone vampire and gave her a look out of blue eyes that said, *Well, what are you waiting for?* It moved back without any direction when one of the uniformed hunters knelt to slip silver handcuffs on the Prime's wrists.

The dog looked familiar, but she couldn't quite place where she'd seen it before. Something about the glinting gold nametag around the dog's neck was also familiar. Its name was Joe.

"Hi, Joe."

He cocked his head at the sound of her voice, but backed away when she would have touched him. Then Joe turned and flashed away, and she left the mystery of the dog to deal with the Prime.

"I think we have proof now that Dawn does send these creatures into psychosis after prolonged use," one of the cops said.

"Yeah," she answered. And wondered what Sid Wolf, who wasn't yet sure Dawn was harmless, would make of this.

She looked around the beach, where a crowd was gathering. "Let's get this one out of here."

Chapter Eleven

By the time Eden returned to the safe house, she was almost at the point of collapse. She'd had a rough night, and a tense morning that had now turned into afternoon. Her butt was dragging, her brain was fried, and she guessed she wasn't cut out for working by night and sleeping by day.

It didn't help that she'd had a fight with the other hunters, which ended with her having to pull rank and point out that she had been put in charge of this operation. That had been after her cousin Charlie pulled out his cell phone to call her father for advice.

That had been after she'd refused to let them kill the captured Tribe Prime when they were done taking samples for testing.

"Are you beginning to believe they're people,

after running with one for a couple of nights?" Charlie had taunted.

"It would have killed that woman," Andre had pointed out.

"Think of it as an injured animal that has to be put down," Charlie said. "If you have to have any sympathy for it at all."

"I want the Prime kept locked up and under constant observation," she'd ordered. "He's a drug addict. It might be useful if we study the effects of the drug and withdrawal. Think of the Prime as a lab rat," she sneered at Charlie. "If you have to have any reasons to follow my orders."

They'd left it at that, with the boys grudgingly obeying. Eden came back to the apartment weary in soul and body and with a blazing headache.

She looked at the tiny tape recorder she'd left sitting on the computer desk, and considered adding to her observations. Not now, she decided. She was in no mood for doing any sort of documentation right now.

But that was a bad and wrong attitude, since she'd made a commitment to this blogging project. So she dutifully picked up the voice-activated recorder. "I'm going to blame Wolf for my grumpiness—because if I have to work twenty-four/seven, I think he should, too." She sighed. "That said, last night had its ups and downs. While we didn't acquire the laptop Wolf thinks the tribe vampires want, we now know that . . ."

She lost her train of thought, and swiped a hand tiredly across her face.

"I'm not sure what we learned. Wolf interrogated a captured member of the Hydra tribe, but I'm not sure he told me everything he learned when he read the other vampire's mind. What I did learn is that there's a hit out on me and I find the Tribes taking it so personally disconcerting even though I know that this sort of behavior is historically accurate. It's one of the earmarks of Tribe behavior. But I find it more scary than I do interesting when I'm the target. I told Wolf I wouldn't use the zapper anymore, but I'm going to have to break that promise, for which I will apologize later. Besides, I hear the shower running, so it's not like I'll be disturbing his sleep. He's had hours to rest, but I haven't had any. If there's Tribe Primes on Dawn hunting for me, I want all the protection I can get while I'm resting. If I turn the zapper on at the lowest setting the worst damage it can do to Wolf is a small headache. I'd warn him, if that didn't mean running the risk of walking in on a naked man—vampire—in the bathroom. I'm not saying I wouldn't mind seeing someone that gorgeous naked, but he might get the idea that my reasons were for prurient more than esthetic appreciation. And he'd be right—but I'd be wrong. Meanwhile, I'm going to get some sleep, knowing I'll be shielded from the vampires hunting me. That said, I'm going to bed."

Tribe boys? They have the same instincts as a greyhound—they see a rabbit, and they run after it.

Laurent remembered telling Eden that the night before, but he didn't know why the words haunted him now, hours after the latest confrontation with his pursuers. He turned off the shower, twisted water out of his long hair, and reached for a towel. He should have felt rested, but he didn't. His bruises were healed. He was fed, he was safe from the sun, and no one had yet traced him.

He had spent several hours pacing, telling himself he wasn't worried about Eden herself, he was worried about the safety of his personal hacker.

He knew she was back now, and wondered why she'd been gone so long. His initial urge was to go to her, but he stopped himself a step away from the bathroom door—because the urge was too powerful.

He wanted to see her face, to hear her voice, to catch her scent and her mental energy. He wanted *her*—and this was exactly the sort of Prime behavior he'd armored himself against all his life.

Tribe members did not let themselves become attached to any female, vampire or mortal. Females were for using. Eden was a female—therefore she was to be used.

"Logic," he murmured.

He closed his eyes and made himself think about the survival logic of being a Tribe Prime. Survival was the whole point.

So, no running naked out into the living room to check up on the woman, who was very good at taking care of herself. Of course, she'd probably find it sexy if he sauntered out with a towel draped around his hips to wish her good day, then yawn fetchingly and flash her a smile. That behavior would be charming, seductive. Obvious, yes, but not threatening. Seducing her was a tool in using her.

"Too late now," he murmured, aware that she was exhausted. He felt her drag off to bed, and once again had to stop himself from heading toward her.

Because his impulse was to comfort, rather than to use.

Bad, Laurent. Never forget that you're a selfish bastard, and proud of it.

With that in mind, he finally stepped out of the bathroom. With a few hours to wait while Eden got her rest and a faint headache growing behind his eyes, Laurent decided to lie down for a while himself.

"Run, little one."

"I'm not little!"

"But you will run."

Laurent backed away into the shadows, away from Justinian's glittering smile, away from the bright eyes. He knew the shadows wouldn't help. But they were all he had.

It took him a moment to realize that he had the darkness, too. He was a vampire as much as they were.

"Run."

This time the voice belonged to Belisarius. His brother. The one who wanted him dead.

"It's only a game, little one," Justinian said. "A training exercise."

But for whom?

He wasn't yet a Prime, but the others were. If he ran, and they caught him—

Belisarius lunged, and Laurent had no more time to think.

He ran. His heart pounded. He was full of screaming terror, but cunning swiftly took the place of thought. The instinct for survival was strong in him.

And he would not let Belisarius win. Never. Never.

"Never!"

The scream drove Eden up out of the bed even before she was awake. Her eyes opened as she stumbled out of her room and down the hall. She was standing outside the vampire's room when the shout came again.

"Never!"

This time it sent a shudder of sympathy through her that brought her fully awake.

"What the—" She scrubbed her hands across her face.

She heard Wolf thrashing around and shouting, clearly having a horrible nightmare.

She opened the door and rushed inside.

He was sitting up in bed, and his eyes were open. His head swiveled toward her when she came in, but she could tell he wasn't seeing her. The pain she saw in those staring eyes—pain that came from deep in his heart—drove her forward.

It wasn't until she was holding him in her arms that she remembered that he was a vampire, and even then, it didn't matter.

His back and shoulders were rigid, hard as stone. For a moment she imagined she was embracing the pale marble of a Renaissance statue. But his skin was warm, almost hot to the touch. Not a statue, but a male breathing in ragged gasps.

She murmured into his ear. Stupid things like, "It's all right. I'm here. It's a dream. Just a bad dream." Though she had no idea what was wrong with him at all. The urge was to comfort in any way she could. Something about his being in pain broke her heart.

"Let me make it better," she crooned. "Let me help."

She didn't think he heard her. At least not the words.

When he finally turned his gaze to hers, his gray eyes seemed almost black, and the pain in them was beyond her understanding.

"I ran away," he said. "It was a game to make me scared, but I ran away instead. I won."

The laugh that came out of him then was so bitter, it hurt her ears.

"He always finds me and drags me back. But I did run away."

She wondered if he was talking to her, or still caught in his nightmare.

"It's not real." She brushed her hands through his long silvery hair, damp with sweat. "You're dreaming."

He took a deep breath. She thought he was going to laugh that horrible laugh again, and couldn't stand it.

So she kissed him.

It felt so right to cover his mouth with hers and try to take his pain away.

Aching pleasure swept through her with hard, insistent heat the moment their lips met. His mouth was hot and hungry, and she wanted him instantly. The connection was far more intense than the two times he'd claimed her lips as a reward. Breathless excitement had stirred in her each time, but this took more than her breath away.

Hurricane-force excitement roared through her as her tongue delved inside his mouth. Thought vanished, leaving simple, urgent need.

He moaned against her mouth and was suddenly holding her tightly. His hand cupped the back of her head as he took control of the kiss.

Of her.

A prick of pain pierced her lower lip and shot heat into her nipples and her belly. A faint taste of hot copper on her tongue sharpened desire even more.

The tenseness in him changed, going from fear to commanding desire with a fluid grace that devastated her senses. One moment he was as still as a statue of a naked god. The next he was a god come to life, his skin satin over hard muscle.

She couldn't keep her hands off him. She stroked his hard belly and wide shoulders, explored the long, lean back and narrow hips. She'd been dying to do this since the moment they met. Now restraint melted like mist.

All she wanted was to touch him, to know him. He lay back on the bed and let her. When she pulled off the T-shirt and underwear she'd worn to bed, he laughed softly, as though the sound came from a great distance. There was no mocking in it, just joy. It was as if he'd been in a dark place, but she'd brought him out of it.

The joy of being alive suddenly permeated the room, and it reached deep inside Eden.

There was something else she wanted inside her as well.

She straddled him and slowly kissed her way down his chest; breathed in the rich masculine scent and absorbed the texture of his skin. She felt his erection press against her rump.

When she would have moved back to settle herself on him, his hands came around her waist. The next thing she knew, she was on her back. He loomed over her, large, male, dangerous. His long silver hair brushed sensually against her breasts, sending flickering fire through her nerve endings.

Then his head swooped down. She saw a flash of fang, and fear surged through her. But he only kissed the tip of her nose. It reminded her that he'd said he liked it, and fear melted into a feeling of being cherished.

The adrenaline rush remained.

It heightened the sensations of his hands on her body. His caresses were gentle, slow and thorough. So were the kisses that accompanied them, on her mouth, her cheeks and throat. He drew blood with one tiny nip, and slowly licked the drop away while she arched in a long, shuddering orgasm.

"Sweet," she murmured, coming down.

His chuckle was soft in her ear, his warm breath tantalizing. "Just getting started."

She lay beneath him, boneless, satiated.

Then the caresses began again and she realized that she was nowhere near satiated.

His mouth was on her breast, his tongue slowly circling the puckered nipple as she languidly combed her fingers through the thick silkiness of his long, long hair. It was unfashionable; it was wonderful.

"I'm still stuck in the eighties, I guess," he said, lifting his head briefly.

She didn't think she'd spoken, and didn't think he'd read her mind. It was the gesture he'd interpreted. Then her thoughts drifted away on a rising tide of sensation. His mouth moved from her breast down to her belly, then lower still.

Her thighs fell open for him. His head dipped between her legs; the touch of his tongue brought heaven. She squirmed and writhed, and came, and came again, going higher each time. She begged him to stop—and to never stop—but the only sounds that came from her were raw moans.

Then he moved up her body and slid deep inside her, wringing another orgasm from her. He groaned as her inner muscles rippled around his thick length.

She almost couldn't bear it when he began to move, thrusting into her hard and fast. It took her breath away; it flamed in her blood and made her think of lava boiling through her veins.

"Who needs volcanoes?" she heard herself say.

From a great distance, she heard him laugh once more. She laughed with him.

For some reason the shared humor joined them together in a way deeper than physical. Not that the physical wasn't marvelous.

Especially when his rhythm increased to the point that sent them both over the edge.

It took her so hard, and Eden was so caught up in the glory of it, that she passed right out.

Chapter Twelve

"*I* have a headache," Laurent murmured.

"You're lucky," Eden mumbled against the vampire's chest. "You've no idea how sore I'm going to be in the morning—evening." With actions came consequences.

"It's already evening."

"Whenever. And I'm the one who's supposed to have the headache—before the deed."

"Right. Shouldn't you be reeling from guilt about now?"

"It is impossible to reel in this position."

He patted her on the back and let his hand slide down to cup her slightly raised butt. "I guess."

She probably looked ludicrous, but she was really comfortable. Her head was resting over his heart, which was beating with a slow, inhuman rhythm that should have been disconcerting, but wasn't. His other arm was around her, strong as a steel band, and his fingers toyed gently with the short hair at the back of her neck.

She didn't know when they'd changed positions, or how long she'd been asleep. She was both weary and rested. It had been a while since she'd been with a man, and the aftermath had never been this good.

As she came more awake, she realized that he was right: this was the time when she should be feeling guilty, or at least chagrined. After all, she'd been trained to resist the seductive blandishments that were second nature to a vampire. She searched her conscience, though not very deeply, and discovered that she was feeling just fine.

"Headache," he repeated. "And I hate to be so impolite as to inquire, but what the hell are you doing in here? Not that I'm complaining—or trying to sound unchivalrous."

Eden lifted her head to look him in the eyes and saw that he was the one who was faintly embarrassed. There was pain there as well, physical and spiritual. But he blinked, and nothing of his soul was showing a moment later.

"You were having a nightmare. Your shouting woke me up," she told him. "I was trying to bring you out of it, and . . . things happened. Don't you remember?"

He gazed into the distance and looked intently thoughtful for a while. A bit of the pain returned to his eyes. "I was having a flashback," he corrected. His hand traced down her back, sending a pleasurable shiver through her. "Thanks for bringing me out of it."

She wondered what sort of memory could have provoked Wolf's tortured reaction.

But before she could, he said, "Don't ask."

"That's not fair."

"Such is life. About this headache—"

Eden sat up, and immediately missed the closeness. She quickly went to the living room and shut off the device on the computer desk. She glanced over her shoulder as she did so, expecting Wolf to follow her and make some accusatory remark. But he remained in the bedroom.

Maybe she'd worn him out. Or maybe it was the headache . . .

Which was her fault. Maybe so was the nightmare.

Now a twist of guilt went through her. Not some residual angst over having had sex with a vampire. Oh, no—despite the rules and regs, she could barely keep from smiling like a cat with cream on her face over that.

But she wasn't smiling when she went back into his bedroom. She realized that she shouldn't go back, and she was well aware of being naked. But she went and stood in the doorway anyway, leaning against it, arms crossed under her breasts. The room itself was dim, but there was light coming in from the hallway, falling across the bed. The nude vampire was sitting with his back propped up by pillows, looking even more glorious than she remembered—and she hadn't exactly been gone that long.

She looked him over, and he looked her over. And she finally dipped her head and said, "Sorry about that."

He rubbed his temples. "I thought we had an agreement about that zapper thing."

It wasn't exactly an accusation, but he definitely didn't sound happy. It made her feel like she'd disappointed him.

"I was scared they'd come and get me," she admitted, knowing this wasn't something a hunter should admit to a vampire. She gestured toward the bed, the movement taking in everything that had happened there. "I was as scared as you were."

She waited for him to deny his own fears, but he was honest enough to keep quiet.

"A couple of nights of fighting vampires got

to me," she went on. "I wanted to sleep feeling safe. So I gave you a headache—and probably your bad dream."

"*I'm* here to keep you safe."

Laurent was totally surprised at the conviction of his words. He *was* disappointed that she hadn't trusted or depended on him. It was like he was channeling the Clan Prime he was pretending to be.

"We're partners," he reminded her.

The words came out of his mouth as if he really meant it, and a part of him panicked. And he'd tasted her when they'd had sex, hadn't he? She already had his blood in her, and now he had hers. That was not supposed to happen! If you tasted a female, you *never* gave her your blood—ever, ever, ever! That led to—

Complications.

He groaned and clutched at his temples.

"Are you okay? How's your head?"

Eden's guilty concern was almost too much for him to bear. When she moved toward him, he should have told her to stay away. But he couldn't do it. He wanted her near him.

It was no more than a drop or two, he reassured himself. Not enough to make a connection.

Because he *really* didn't want to have to kill her.

Luckily she wasn't in the least bit psychic, so forming a connection between them would take more than just sharing blood once or twice, right?

He could only guess at how long it took for— he mentally gritted his teeth—*a bond* to form. This was the sort of information Clan and Family Primes were given as they reached puberty— they probably had mortal/vampire sex ed classes. Tribe Primes were only taught how to use blood sharing and torture to turn mortals into blood slaves.

He didn't want a slave. And a bondmate was out of the question. He wasn't even sure which behavior was sicker: bonding or breaking. But bonding was *certainly* a sign of weakness.

But you've always been weak, the memory of Justinian's voice whispered in his mind.

"We can't get involved," he said as she sat on the edge of the bed. Yet even as he spoke, he reached out to touch her. *Weak.*

It was just the merest fingertip caress down the length of her arm. He relished the gesture, though he didn't mean to do it. The texture of her warm, sleek skin rattled him with instant desire.

Somehow their fingers ended up twined together, hands resting on the rumpled sheet. He liked being spoiled, so taking his hand away took more effort than it would have taken one of the good guys.

"I'm sorry, Eden."

He supposed that to her he sounded like a self-sacrificing Clan prig, because the smile she turned on him was rich with irony. "You just said that we're partners."

"You're naked," he pointed out.

Raising one eyebrow, she looked him over slowly and deliberately. For the first time in his life, he blushed, and he was all too aware of a growing erection.

He flipped the edge of a sheet over his hips— not that this hid anything, with the way the cloth tented up over his erection.

She looked at his modestly covered crotch and grinned. That was the last thing he expected from the tough vampire hunter. But it wasn't like he'd hypnotized her into wanting him. Maybe she just wanted him because she *wanted* him. What was humming between them had nothing to do with psychic energy.

"Madam," he said. "You are taking advantage of my vulnerable—"

"Do you know how positively Victorian you sound?"

"Do you know how positively glorious your breasts are?"

Screw it!

He pulled her forward and buried his face between her glorious breasts. Why was he trying to think when there was an obviously willing female on the bed?

He spent the next few minutes exploring Eden's breasts, before she pulled back the sheet and took his cock in her hand.

"Oh, yeah," he murmured, and leaned back and closed his eyes.

This was pure, simple sex. Sharing pleasure on this basic level couldn't get either of them into trouble.

Her mouth dipped to cover the tip of his penis. Her tongue swirled, and he groaned.

"You like this," she said.

Oh, yes, he liked it very much.

For a while he rode the sensations as she stroked and sucked him from base to tip, over and over again. The whole world centered on the way she was bringing him to the edge.

When he was nearly ready to explode, she changed positions. Her hand still grasped his cock, but only until she guided him inside her. She took him in slowly, buried him in soft, wet heat, surrounded him.

Completed him.

Damn.

He put one hand on her hip to steady her and found her breasts with the other. *Sensation. Just go with sensation.*

He stroked her thighs and her belly and her fine, firm ass as she rode him, in awe of every inch of her sweet curves and hard muscles. She controlled this ecstasy, and he let her. She did what she wanted, and everything she wanted brought him pleasure.

"That's right, have your way with me, you wicked wench."

She laughed, the sound breathless and sexy. Then her breath caught, and her back arched, and he felt the orgasm ripple through her all along the length of his shaft, taking him up over the edge. The explosive release left him dumb and blind.

And for a moment, completely happy.

Chapter Thirteen

"This was a bad idea." She was still resting on top of him, her forehead on his chest. He didn't know how long they'd been like this. Her voice was muffled, but he had no trouble understanding her. "I am such a fool."

He patted her shoulder, but didn't offer any reassurance. "Yes."

She lifted her head and met his gaze with a glare. "Protection," she said. "Why the hell didn't one of us think of using protection? Do you have any condoms on you?"

Apparently she wasn't thinking along the same lines as he was. About this, he could reassure her. "It's okay. Do you know how long it takes a vampire to get a mortal pregnant?"

"Once."

Shock ran through him, and he sputtered, "But—no—it doesn't—I don't think it works like that."

"Has anyone told you about the birds and bees?"

Laurent took a deep breath as she looked at him accusingly. Her chin was resting on his breastbone, and the sensation was rather sharp. He thought this might be what a stake poised over his heart might feel like.

"Has anyone told you about vampires and mortals?" he ventured.

"I am a trained vampire hunter," she pointed out. "Who is royally ignoring her training," she added, and kissed the spot above his heart.

"We have to talk about that, Eden."

She nodded. "As soon as you convince me I'm not going to get in the family way."

He ruffled her hair. "Not likely. Mortals have to be bonded to a vampire for that."

"I drank your blood." She looked thoughtful, and added, "I think you drank mine."

"A drop or two."

She looked horrified for a flash of a second. "That doesn't mean we're bonded, does it?"

It was good to know that she was as opposed to the idea of bonding as he was. At least that was something the Tribes and the hunters had in common. Okay, there was a part of his ego—or maybe it was Prime instinct—that believed, deep down, that bonding with him was something this mortal should be eager for. Which was such a load of crap.

"Bonding can take years. What do they teach you about vampire and human sex at hunter school, anyway?"

She blushed and momentarily looked away. When she looked back, there was a mischievous sparkle in her eyes. "We're told not to, of course. You," she reminded him, "are a monster."

"I am," he agreed.

"We are also told that temptation is inevitable, but must be resisted."

He grinned smugly. "You seemed to have flunked that class."

"I'll get back to resisting you later."

He ran his hands over her back. She reacted by arching her back, and the movement caused his penis to grow hard, pressing tightly between their bodies. She shifted a little, arousing him more.

He let his breath out in a long whoosh. "Woman, are we going to start all over again?"

She grinned. "Feels like it."

He rolled them over, putting her under him. "You are insatiable."

"Isn't that supposed to be my line?"

She traced his lips with a fingertip, the touch

maddeningly seductive. Then she pulled his head to hers for a fierce, possessive kiss. All Laurent could do was lose himself again in the wanting. And in the having.

Eden had no idea what time it was. It felt like she'd been asleep for hours.

She was thoroughly rested, yet she didn't want to move. The bed was comfortable, and the warm, hard body wrapped around hers provided secure contentment she'd never felt before.

That she'd never felt this contented feeling with a man before disturbed her. But he wasn't a man—though he was very male.

She was going to have to get up soon. Physical necessity needed to be met. And she was going to have to get back to work. Eden sighed. Though she'd done it under protest, she had taken on the responsibility of running this op.

"You just didn't know how hard it was really going to be," Wolf whispered in her ear.

"Are you reading my mind?"

"Body language."

She suspected this wasn't quite true, but let it go. "I'm more of a computer geek than a commando. Though I shouldn't be admitting that to a big, bad Clan Prime."

He gave a snort of laughter and kissed her

ear. "Being a commando isn't my day job, either, sweetie. You learn to fight when you have to," he added. "And you're pretty good at it."

She chose to take this as a compliment, because he probably did mean it that way. And it was good to know that he found her competent.

She rolled out of his grasp and off the bed. "I'm getting out of the hunter business when this is over," she announced, and then left the room.

"Poor kid," Laurent said when she was gone.

The fact that he really meant it scared him. *Claustrophobia.* He'd been in one place too long, with one woman, carrying out a disguise that admittedly carried a certain amount of temptation.

What he'd needed—what he'd always needed—was a life to call his own.

And that's where Eden really comes in. A means to an end.

He got up and followed his means to an end to the bathroom, where the shower was running.

When he got in with her, he said, "No shower sex, I promise."

"Too bad." She pressed her back and buttocks against him. Her skin was warm and slick, fragrant with jasmine soap.

He put his hands on her shoulders, moving her so that they weren't so tightly pressed together. He wasn't sure if the steam surrounding them was from the water, or coming off their skins. He took a deep breath.

"Showering together is simply more efficient. But I will scrub your back," he added when she gave him a skeptical look over her shoulder.

He ended up washing her hair as well. And from the look of pleasure on her face as he massaged her scalp, that was almost as good as sex.

"Another cup?" Wolf asked.

"Sure."

Eden was surprised he was asking for coffee, and that made her realize she was getting used to the sight of his drinking blood. Another way of letting her hunter's guard down.

She poured, and glanced at the clock on the microwave before putting down the carafe. It was nearly eleven in the morning. She was fairly certain that it was Monday. She was finally rested, and she hadn't realized just how badly she needed it until now.

"Living by night is not my thing. How can you stand it?" she asked the vampire.

He was leaning back against the kitchen counter, looking relaxed and refreshed in tight black trousers and T-shirt. His damp hair was tightly braided.

She remembered it hanging long and loose in a silver cloud around his face, and the ache for him knotted deep inside her. She'd been careful not to touch him since they'd stepped out of the shower and gone to separate rooms to dress.

Thinking about his hair reminded her of the comment he'd made about the eighties. He'd probably been hanging out at the Roxy while she was in grade school. She considered age differences, and how deceptive it was that vampires looked so young.

He smiled. "How do we stand living by night? It is our natural state, remember. Our children are raised in the dark, like mushrooms. Even the ones who use the daylight drugs can't take them until they're adults."

That reminded her of the vampires they'd taken down—yesterday? Hell, she should have followed up on it hours ago.

"We've been distracted," she told her partner. "Which was my fault, and I apo—"

"Not again," he warned. He put his mug on the counter. "You have something you want to tell me?"

She nodded. "There were a pair of Manti-core Primes having psychotic episodes yesterday morning down by—"

"Manticores?" He shook his head. "Justinian wouldn't allow his Primes to use drugs."

His fierce certainty rattled Eden. "They *were* Manticores. We tested the one we caught—"

"Only one?" He looked disgusted.

"Let me finish. This Manticore was using Dawn."

"How do you know he's a Manticore?"

"He told us. Actually, he threatened us with Justinian's ire at daring to hold a Prime, blah, blah, blah. But you can read his mind if you want to check for yourself."

"No need. Nobody's going to claim to be one of Justinian's if he isn't. But I can't see Justinian letting his boys use Dawn. That would loosen his control of them."

"Who says they asked permission?"

He opened his mouth to answer, then closed it after a moment. He looked bewildered, and bemused, then he shrugged. "That's just a weird concept for me." He gave a mirthless chuckle. "Though I'm the last person who should be sur-prised by that."

"Why?"

"Manticores by daylight, eh?"

His evasiveness left her wondering if he had some personal knowledge of Justinian. She recalled his waking nightmare words—*It was a game to make me scared, but I ran away*—with an awful suspicion that couldn't possibly be correct. Those had been the words of a terrified child, and the Clans were fiercely protective of their young.

"Up to no good, as Manticores usually are," she answered, dismissing her suspicions.

"What did they do?"

"They didn't actually get around to attacking anyone," she admitted, "but the one we caught was chasing a woman. Somehow I doubt he was trying to ask her for her phone number."

"It's possible that using the drug had nothing to do with why they were acting out," he suggested. "Maybe their weird behavior had nothing to do with the drug."

"I really don't follow you, Wolf."

"You asked how we can stand living by night—but if living in the dark is all you know from birth, adjusting to daylight has to be traumatic. Maybe what you hunters have been assuming is psychotic—because goodness knows, vampires are primed to turn violent at any moment—is actually a reaction to a new way of sensing the world."

"It's still dangerous," she pointed out. "That's why you Clans and Families supervise the transition, right?"

He didn't look happy at her reasoning, but grudgingly said, "Yeah. I suppose."

"Suppose?" His diffidence made her angry. "Right. You don't *do* daylight. That's why we're stuck in here for the rest of the day."

In reality, she was mad at herself for all the time she'd taken away from the job. The quirked eyebrow and half-smile he gave her told her that he was well aware of where her true annoyance lay.

"You can leave at any time, Faveau," he reminded her.

"Yeah." But the truth was, she didn't want to be away from him—which was bad for the op. And worse for her emotional well-being. "I should go check in with my people and find out the test results. Then pick up some groceries and stuff."

These things could be done with a couple of phone calls. But it would be good for her to get away from Sid Wolf for a while.

He gestured toward the door. "You go to work, sweetheart." The grin he gave her was totally mischievous, totally devastating. "I'll stay home and watch Spanish soap operas."

Chapter Fourteen

Joe Bleythin went up the walk to the rambling stucco house that held Bleythin Investigations with reluctance. He used to look forward to coming to work. To a job worth doing, and doing it with thoroughness and pride. He'd been honored to learn the business.

And, the pay was good.

They were private detectives, but they didn't take just any cases. No following cheating spouses for divorce cases—his elder twin brothers Harrison and Michael founded the business strictly as a missing-persons agency. As the family joke went, they had a "nose" for it.

Right now Joe was in the mood for chucking it all in and finding something less stressful to do with his time. Like chasing rabbits, maybe. Or going back to the Air Force.

He stepped up to the door and walked in, because he was the boss at the moment. The main room was large, containing three desks and a lot of other office paraphernalia. A picture window looked out on the desert landscaped lawn and busy street beyond. Doors led to two other offices, and a long hallway went to the private areas in the back of the building.

Two people were already in the room, and they looked at him as he entered—the male in mild surprise, the female in faint annoyance.

"What? Am I late?"

Joe would have checked his watch, had it not been stolen from the café bathroom the day before. At least his clothes were still there when he got back from the vampire chase. He'd learned never to take a wallet with him. He'd only lost about ten dollars in cash, and thieves never took the car key he carried.

All in all, yesterday morning had been pretty weird.

"Sid in yet?" he asked the annoyed office manager.

Cathy Carter bared her teeth at him in a snarl.

"Hey! What'd I do?"

"You're being insensitive," Daniel Corbett said.

He was seated in the chair next to Sid's desk.

Typically, he had a cup of coffee in one hand and a book in the other. Daniel didn't technically work for the agency, but he was around so much, Joe figured they should either pay him a salary or start charging him rent. He was a cousin of Sid's, the result of crossbreeding between a vampire and a human; scarily brilliant and weirdly psychic, but otherwise a fairly normal mortal—for a geek.

A geek who was looking disapprovingly at Joe over the top of his glasses.

Then it occurred to Joe why Cathy was in such a foul mood. He'd been born a werewolf, so he didn't pay much attention to the phases of the moon. Cathy was one of the unfortunate victims of a werewolf gone bad; a bite from an attacker had brought her over to the wolf side. It took years for a human who'd been turned to get control over their morphing abilities, and the full moon played hell with their lives. Cathy was entering the time of month where she'd be spending four days locked up in the padded and soundproofed back room.

She hated that they had to get a temp in once a month to mess with her well-organized office.

"Sid's not in, and I have a lot to do," she growled.

"Sorry. I'll leave you alone."

"You do that."

He carefully didn't show any annoyance at being even more short-staffed in the days ahead. It wasn't Cathy's fault some crazy bastard had taken a bite out of her, left her for dead, but turned her, instead. His brother Mike had found the bastard and made sure he never victimized another human. It was Mike who'd brought Cathy home.

And right now Mike was another missing member of the agency's staff. Not that Joe was going to complain about Michael Bleythin checking himself into rehab. He hadn't fallen off the wagon, but he had been having *urges*.

"And there's nothing meaner than a drunken werewolf," Joe muttered as he settled behind his own desk.

"Don't talk bad about your brother," Cathy called from across the room.

Blast and dang werewolf hearing! "It was a statement of fact," he replied.

"He had to kill another feral," Cathy said. "You know what that does to him."

Mike could do no wrong in Cathy's eyes—but he was the only person who couldn't. If Joe were to complain about Harry's neglecting the family business to spend too much time with his new wife in Arizona, Cathy would agree with him.

She'd not only agree, but launch into a lecture on how it was not only a bad idea, but downright wrong for a werewolf to have married a human. Cathy was recently converted to the shapeshifter way of life, and in the way of new converts, she was somewhat fanatical about ancient tradition.

The root of Joe's frustration lay in the fact that his brothers were not around. And it wasn't only because werewolves were pack creatures. Joe was way too overworked, and beginning to feel out of control. This was not a state he thrived in.

On top of that, now there was something going on in the vampire community, and he strongly suspected he was going to get more involved in it. The drugged-out Primes he'd encountered yesterday must have something to do with the hunter/Clan operation Sid had turned over to a relative.

He checked e-mail and voice mail, but there were no messages from either of his brothers or Sid Wolf. "Guess I'm on my own. What are you doing here, Daniel? And would you like a job?"

"Waiting for Sid." He nudged the antique Murano glass paperweight on Sid's desk out of the way to make room for his coffee cup. "I'd love to help you find missing persons, Joe. That's why I'm waiting for Sid."

Daniel had a strong psychic gift, but it wasn't much use for anything practical. Daniel Corbett could visualize the person who'd last been in a place, or held an object, and tell you all about them with frightening accuracy. If the person had lived a thousand or two years ago, that is. Daniel put his talent to use as an historian, or tried to. His colleagues in academia tended to think of him as a crank and a nutjob when he couldn't provide actual hard evidence for the things he *knew.*

Sid had been teaching him how to focus his gifts on reading more modern objects. So far Daniel had managed to work his way up to occasionally seeing visions from about fifty years in the past. If he ever made it up to the here and now, he would be an invaluable asset to the missing persons firm.

"While you are good company," Joe said to Daniel, "you take up valuable space."

"And drink too much of your coffee," Daniel agreed. "Go chase your tail," he added, and went back to reading his book.

Joe pulled up a file and began to type, but his phone rang before he could type more than a few words. Joe felt a moment of dread before the second ring sounded. He trusted his instincts and hesitated to answer. But on the third ring, he picked it up.

The caller was Sid's mother, Lady Antonia. And, sure enough, there was trouble.

Warning bells in his head urged Laurent to leave, and he paced the apartment, longing for the night. He'd gotten away with playing a Clan boy for three days, and it was bound to fall apart soon. He needed to make escape plans.

But you had to work with what the fates gave you, and they'd given him Eden. The worst part of it was, he wanted to keep her. Such insanity had to be nipped in the bud.

Nipping. He smiled. He liked the idea of nipping Ms. Eden Faveau. Often. It made his fangs ache just thinking about it. Thinking about it too much would make him hard, as well.

You really only need her for one thing, he reminded himself sternly. And sex isn't it.

Still, he closed his eyes and instantly saw her naked. With her clothes on she appeared rather angular, almost gawky. But naked, oh, my, the treasures that were revealed. He liked her back, and the way it tapered down to the lovely round curve of her ass. He liked her strong arms and legs. Her limbs were long and supple and nicely muscled. Her belly had just the right feminine curve. Her hips were a bit narrow, but maybe after she had a kid—

Whoa—what darkly wholesome part of his imagination had *that* thought bubbled up from?

He also liked being with her, and he wasn't supposed to like being with people. Not that he liked being with his own kind. Who *was* he supposed to like being with?

Well, he did like Eden naked, and that was acceptable. If he decided to keep her—own her—he'd keep her naked all the time.

That was a much better thought for a Tribe Prime.

He checked the clock, though he didn't need to. Awareness of the movements of light and dark was born in him. Did that sense dull in those who used the daylight drugs? Maybe he'd get his hands on a dose of Dawn and find out for himself.

Should he use Eden to help him acquire the Dawn as well as break into the Patron's computer? No. That was an excuse to stay around her longer. He knew who to go to for the drug, but that would wait until after he'd acquired the Patron's wealth. He could have anything he wanted, then.

Trying to cure his restlessness, he sat down at the computer. He had no clue how to get online, but he did discover the PC version of Escape from Butcher Bay, so he played the computer game for a couple of hours.

As sunset neared, Eden still wasn't back. He'd been mentally searching the whole time he'd been playing, hunting for any vampires in the area. Even with the nasty zapper thing off, the safe house seemed to still be clear. Several nights of fights and an apparent bad reaction to Dawn had thinned the ranks of Manticores.

It was time for him to venture out on the streets alone. He needed to stretch his legs. He needed the fresh air.

He needed to retrieve the laptop, and he was tired of his Clan-boy impersonation delaying that.

He stood and dug a coin out of his pocket. Heads, he'd leave Eden a note. Tails, he'd do what a Prime should—go about his business without regard to some lowly female's sensibilities.

The toss came out tails.

Chapter Fifteen

"How nice to see you." There was acid in the sweet tone of her aunt's voice.

"Hello, Aunt Michele."

She wanted to ask, *how'd you find me?* And, *what are you doing here?* But it was known in the family that this was her favorite coffee shop in a small open air mall near the condo development that was her real home.

Aunt Michele was called in when total psychological domination was called for.

"Here for an intervention, are you?" Eden asked.

She was already annoyed with the rest of the hunter team, and now this. A lot of progress had been made on the Dawn problem, but to hear the rest of the team tell it, she was somehow being corrupted—going soft—by having spent a couple of days in the company of Sid Wolf.

"That, and a latte," her aunt answered, sitting opposite her in the coffee shop's back booth. She eyed the shopping bags next to Eden. "Isn't Bosworth's a men's store?"

"Yes, Aunt Michele."

While her aunt's tone hadn't exactly been accusing, Eden hated that her answer had been accompanied by a twinge of guilt. What did she have to be guilty for?

"Are you running errands for one of *them* now?"

This time Aunt Michele's tone was distinctly more hostile, and there was a disappointed look in her eyes. Her father's sister, Michele Darabont, was not officially a Purist—the radical sect of vampire killers the hunters officially disavowed. But rumor had it that she was in contact with the leaders of the Purist fanatics, and she certainly didn't disagree with their agenda.

"We're working out of the safe house. He didn't have a chance to bring any clothes with him."

"This—person—has a lair," Michele pointed out. "Contacts of his own. Your serving him like this is just the sort of thing they expect."

"I picked up a few things on my own initiative. He didn't ask me for anything."

Aunt Michele was silent while a very large cup of coffee with a high head of frothed milk was set before her and the waitress moved out of earshot. She glared reprovingly at Eden, who glared right back, refusing to flinch.

"He'll accept what you offer as though it's his right, and you'll get used to his high-handed behavior. Perhaps you already are. They're insidious and subtle. They don't even notice their own arrogance because, after all, they are Prime." She snorted derisively. "Prime users. Prime takers."

"I've heard this lecture all my life, Aunt Michele. I know the drill."

"But this is the first time any of our own have had to deal face-to-face with them for an extended time. Remember your training. Believe what I tell you now."

This was getting old. And very, very annoying. "Wolf's helping us."

"For his own purposes. His loyalty is to his Clan."

"I understand that. But as long as the problem is solved, and no humans get hurt, who cares?"

Besides, the hunters were working with the vampires for their own purposes, too. Nobody's motives were clean and pure. Keeping the Tribes in line served both sides of the alliance. Eden couldn't recall if she'd been a narrow-minded idealist like her aunt before actually getting her hands bloody with fieldwork, but she was certainly more of a pragmatist now. Getting to know Wolf was part of her changing attitude, of course, but not all of it. Yet any deviation from the party line would now be blamed on the vampire. He was the big, bad Wolf in their eyes.

Michele took a sip of latte, then wiped froth off her mouth with a napkin. "You're starting to like him."

It was not a question, and not *exactly* an accusation.

Eden admitted to herself that she'd started liking Wolf from the time they'd had a conversation in this same coffee shop a few nights ago. He challenged her assumptions, made her think outside the box. Not just about vampires, but about her life, and the things she wanted to do with it. They made a good team. She trusted him in a fight.

"He saved my life."

And he was fantastic in bed.

Which was the last thing she'd tell any other hunter; especially not a relative.

"Am I still in charge of this operation?" She already knew the answer to that, because she knew tradition as well as her aunt did, but it was time to clarify the point.

"I can't relieve you. Only your father can do that."

"But you did call him, right?"

"He asked me to talk to you. You spent a lot of time alone with the vampire yesterday. That has us all worried."

"We were working." Eden could almost hear Wolf say, *That's my story and I'm sticking to it,* which made her smile.

Which, of course, made her aunt frown even more.

"Do you know what I was doing when you showed up?" Eden asked. "I was thinking very hard about what needs to be done to keep my emotions neutral here, and the partnership professional. I've been thinking about this stuff for hours. I'm not about to go over to the Dark Side, Aunt Michele."

She wasn't. She hoped.

Her attraction to Wolf was strong, and on many levels, but she was going to fight it. She'd been giving herself reasons for not wanting him to touch her, trying to forget the texture of his lips, the precise warmth and weight of his hands on her breasts.

"He'll be gone soon anyway," she reminded

both herself and her anxious relative. Eventually she'd forget his smile, his laughter, his sarcastic comments and challenging opinions. "Once this op is over, I don't plan on dealing with vampires ever again."

Michele looked somewhat relieved. "Then you don't mind my reinforcing what you've already worked out?"

"Yes, I do." Eden tempered her annoyance with a smile. She also managed not to grit her teeth when she added, "But I do appreciate your concern."

Michele relaxed and nodded. She sipped her latte, Eden finished her fourth cup of coffee, and an almost comfortable silence reigned until they were done.

As it turned out, Daniel's presence in the office was useful. He could drive a car, which was something Joe couldn't do while morphed into wolf form. He needed to be in wolf form to find a trail, so he'd brought Daniel along with him on his hunt.

He decided to go wolf after they'd checked Sid's house and several hangouts, but found nothing out of the ordinary, or a scent new enough to pursue. Fortunately, he knew that there was one trail he might be able to pick up.

Not only had Sid not shown up for work, but the august Lady Antonia was very worried about Sid's not having been at the Clan compound over the weekend.

According to Antonia, the Clan didn't know anything about an agreement to work with vampire hunters. Joe had agreed to look into it discreetly instead of Antonia asking any Primes for help. The lady and he agreed that it was better for him to find his partner than for the matter to exacerbate tensions that already existed within the clan over Sid's lifestyle.

"It's your car, shed on the upholstery if you want," Daniel commented when they headed for the beach.

Joe bared his impressive set of fangs in response, but Daniel ignored the threat.

That was one of the problems with people who spent time around werewolves—not that there were many, either human, vampire, or other, who knew about werefolk. But those who did tended to have this sense of security that their dear friends wouldn't hurt them in morphed form. It was mostly true, but not always, and Joe felt shapeshifters ought to receive more respect from the monoform population.

After a few seconds in the front seat of the

convertible, Joe forgot about being disgruntled and let his most basic instincts take over. Strongest of all was the sense of smell, and Joe loved the way the city smelled.

Unlike most werewolves, Joe had been born and bred in an urban environment. Most came into cities only when they had to. But the Bleythin boys made the streets and alleys, with all the grunge and grit and garbage, their playground. It took him a while to get his mind on the job, what with all the myriad layers of aroma to explore and sort out, but Joe's human brain wasn't needed for a while anyway.

By the time they reached the scene of the vampire weirdness, Joe had his mind on business and was ready to work. Because of where they were, he allowed Daniel to hold one end of a long leash until they got down to the beach. He didn't mind that people always ooohed and aahhed and stopped to ask what kind of dog he was; it was all part of undercover work. And better to be looked at as a large dog—most people guessed some kind of malamute/Newfoundland mix—than to be suspected of being any kind of wolf.

Once they were at the spot where he'd knocked down the vampire, Joe tugged the leash out of Daniel's hand and put his nose to the sand. The remnant presence of the crazy vampire didn't interest him, but the humans who had taken it away certainly did. Especially the woman. He'd recognized her as the one who'd been in the car with the Clan Prime. If he tracked her down, odds were he'd find the Prime Sid had handed the Dawn job. Which might lead him to Sid.

Sorting out the mass of scents that had been laid over the site since the day before was very difficult, but a faint impression finally emerged from the morass.

Joe looked up to find Daniel staring off at the water a distance away, and howled to get his attention. That got a *lot* of people's attention, but he wouldn't have barked even if he knew how. He *was* a werewolf; he had his pride. The howl brought the absentminded professor running, but Joe moved much faster and was waiting in the car when Daniel came pelting up, all breathless and sweaty.

"You need more exercise," Joe observed.

"You need to put some clothes on," Daniel answered.

Joe shrugged. "I have a towel in my lap."

He stayed in human form only long enough to give Daniel directions, then scrunched down in the front seat and morphed, to make it easier to catch the scent again. Running off on his own without a human helper would have been best, but it didn't do for a huge black wolf to be seen roaming the streets in daylight. It was not safe, especially for the wolf.

Tracking the scent took them through a lot of twists and turns, and Joe had to morph several times to give verbal directions, since neither he nor Daniel could communicate telepathically. It was after dark by the time they reached their destination, an ordinary apartment building. Joe had a multiple-morphing headache bad enough to make him want to snap something's head off. God help any rat that wandered out of an alley tonight.

After a thorough reconnoiter he sent Daniel home and settled down behind a thick row of bushes to wait. He was certain that this was the right place. He was equally certain that neither the woman nor the vampire was in the building. The vampire hadn't been gone long, and Joe considered following him. But something told him to wait, and he trusted his senses.

Sure enough, he hadn't been crouched in the bushes for long when the woman's car turned into the building's parking lot. She had to stop to punch in a code to open the entrance doorway. Joe took a chance and trotted out to sit in front of the black VW Bug, directly in the glare of the headlights.

She noticed him and immediately opened the door and got out.

"Hi, Joe. What are you doing here?"

Good. She remembered him. She was also smart enough to keep the open car door between herself and the large animal in her way. She'd seen him knock a vampire to the ground. If she had a weapon, though, she didn't go for it.

Joe looked at her like a pup begging for food and tilted his head to one side, at the precise angle to produce maximum adorability.

"Okay, you're very cute. What do you want?" she asked.

He'd shown himself, he'd made himself look submissive. What more could he do? He stood and turned toward the garage entrance, pointing his elegant long snout at the door. He supposed he could whine and scratch at it, but that was going a bit overboard.

She grinned. "What is it, Lassie? Do you want the vampire? Is that it, girl?"

He growled low in the throat, and hoped she didn't hear it. He turned back to her.

As he did, she slid back into the driver's seat. Before he could spring after her, she reached over and opened the passenger door. He didn't hesitate to jump into the car. She punched in her entry code and drove into the garage.

"I don't know why I'm doing this," she said as she drove to an empty parking space.

She reached over and scratched between his ears. He leaned into her touch, not only to continue reassuring her that he was safe, but because it felt really good.

When she took some bags out of the back seat and got out of the car, he jumped out behind her. He trotted beside her into the elevator.

"I hope you aren't a barker," she said when the door closed. "Because we aren't supposed to have animals in the building. I mean, having a vampire in residence is bad enough, but the neighbors would really complain about a dog—except that you aren't a dog, are you? I know a wolf when I see one. After looking at you for a while, that is."

Okay, first off, she talked to animals. A lot of people did that, so it wasn't too strange that she was holding a one-sided conversation with him. Secondly, she took him for a wolf, and wasn't in the least bit afraid. Why?

He nudged her thigh, and she understood it for a question.

"Sid's from the Wolf Clan." She rubbed his

head again. "So I guess that's who you belong to, right, Joe?"

Belong? His head came up, but he managed not to snarl at the woman. And in a way, she was sort of right. Long ago in the bad old days, when humans hunted them regularly, the Clans and the werefolk had made an alliance to help and protect each other. This had come to be known as the Affiliation, and werewolves naturally tended to run with the Wolf Clan. Which was one reason Sid was his partner.

When they reached the apartment, he wasn't sure what to do. He already knew the vampire was gone. And he wasn't going to morph back to human form in front of someone he didn't yet trust, simply for the sake of holding a proper conversation. But he wanted to find out what his nose could tell him.

So he followed her in and let her shut the door, though it gave him the feeling of being caged.

She put her bags down and called, "Wolf!"

Of course there was no answer. Joe found it odd that humans couldn't tell when they were alone. It was sheer numbers that made them kings of the world, because most of them didn't have any useful senses to write home about.

"Wolf?"

The small living room held a computer setup that looked like it could be used to control missions to Mars. She picked up a pad of yellow paper that had been left on the desk chair.

"Looks like he left me a note." She glanced at it and chuckled. "It says he wasn't going to leave a note, but decided not to worry me."

She sounded charmed, and her body chemistry changed subtly in response to thinking about the vampire. *So you're turned on by this Wolf, Joe* thought. *But what does the note say? Any mention of Sid?*

Her cell phone rang, and she put down the pad to answer it. "Wolf? What's that noise?"

"I could use a little help, sweetheart," Joe heard the vampire answer.

"On my way. Where are you?"

"About three blocks west of the alley where we first met. On a warehouse roof."

"Stay put. Should I bring Joe?"

"Let's leave the team out of it. Hold on." There was a whoosh sound, then a shout. "I like this crossbow. Come alone. Hurry."

"Stay," the woman ordered Joe. She snatched a piece of equipment off the desk and left.

Once she was out the door, he morphed back to human form. "You kids have fun," he murmured, and flexed his fingers. It was good to have thumbs again. He scratched his chest, yawned, and proceeded to have a thorough look around the apartment.

He was intrigued when he found the small tape recorder on the desk. He was even more intrigued when he rewound it and began to listen.

Chapter Sixteen

Laurent jumped off the roof as the VW pulled up to the curb. His ankles twinged a bit when he landed on the hard concrete but he was otherwise fine, as it was only a three-story drop.

Fine was not a word that could be used for the two Manticore Primes he'd left with hawthorn wood arrows sticking out of their chests up on the flat roof of the building. Why wouldn't they just leave him alone?

Oh, yeah, the computer.

He pulled open the passenger door and tossed the laptop case into the back seat.

At last! He had the computer, retrieved from its hiding space in the aerospace museum. He was going to be rich! Even better, he was going to be free.

Laurent slid in beside Eden and grabbed her

for a hard kiss. The taste of her sent his blood zinging, adding to his excitement.

"What took you so long?"

"Traffic."

"Thanks for the pickup." He threw his head back and cackled with glee. "Drive, my beauty. Drive."

She gave him a quick, worried look. "You feeling all right?"

He patted her knee, then stroked farther up her shapely thigh. Her skin was warm, wonderful. "I've never felt better in my life. And you feel damn good yourself."

She squirmed under his touch. "You're distracting me."

"You want to pull over and fool around?"

She laughed, but her attention was on the rearview mirror.

Laurent sighed. He didn't have to look. He could feel them. "We're being followed." He closed his eyes and concentrated. After a few moments, he said, "Hydras this time. The Manticores want me; the Hydras want you. We're a very popular couple."

"In all the wrong circles." She gently pushed his hand away from her thigh. "It's enough to make a girl want to stay home, with the zapper on and the covers pulled up over her head."

"Not you," he said, and put his hand on her shoulder this time. "You live for action, adventure, all that hunter stuff."

"And you are Prime," she answered, mockingly sententious. "Born to save the world."

"Whether it wants to be saved or not."

They shared a sardonic look and a moment of perfect understanding.

Then he remembered that he wasn't really a Prime of Clan Wolf. So the moment was a lie. And the lie twisted like a knife in his heart.

Weird.

Laurent forced the pain away, but not before she noticed the change in him.

"What's the matter? Are you hurt?"

Her concern didn't help, so he concentrated on the situation.

"What shall we do about your Hydras?"

"Track them down to their lair and destroy them utterly?" she suggested brightly.

"That could be fun," he agreed. "But I meant the ones behind us."

"Lair's a silly word, isn't it?" she added.

"Right now I'd like to get back to ours. This could be a problem, since they have a telepathic fix on us."

"I was thinking about that," she answered. She jerked a thumb toward the back seat. "We can be rid of them, if you don't mind having a brief headache."

He glanced behind her. The zapper was resting next to his precious laptop.

"It's not hooked to a power source," he tried hopefully.

"It runs on batteries as well as current."

Great, the hunters had a portable anti-vampire weapon. "I hate we've all gone so high-tech," he complained. "What happened to using our wits?"

"You mean your superior speed and strength against our primitive weapons?"

"And cunning," he added. "We all used to use cunning."

"Quit stalling. I can spend the rest of the night trying to outrun these guys, or we can disorient them and head back to base."

He sighed. He wanted to see what was in the laptop. "Okay, we'll use the zapper. But if I go psycho violent on your ass, it's your fault."

"You won't."

She sounded way too confident, way too trusting. "I might," he warned her.

"You'll have to work the controls," she told him. "There's a timer control, so you can send out a brief pulse. We've never tried using it this way. In fact, we weren't sure it would actually work until—"

"You tortured me with it?"

"Oh, don't be such a baby. It's meant to blank out telepathy, not hurt anybody."

He let it go, and pulled the zapper into his lap.

Headlights were coming up fast behind them now.

"I think they're going to ram us." Eden's foot pressed down on the accelerator, and her tricked-out little Volkswagen flew down the street. She gained a block on their pursuers in a few seconds, and barely made it through a changing light at a busy intersection as it went from yellow to red. "That won't hold them for long," she told him. "Hurry up and figure out the controls. Set it for ten seconds. No, twenty."

He studied the zapper. "Got it."

She slowed the car to let the vampires get closer. "Go."

He pressed a button.

Blinding pain roared through his head. The crash of metal screamed in his ears, while a scream of agony tore from his throat. He had to get away. Had to escape.

Had to.

He had no control over his claws, or his fangs, or his muscles.

The pain—

"Now, that didn't hurt too much, did it?"

Laurent became slowly aware of the night, of the shredded upholstery, of his claws still buried in the dashboard, of the machine that was now lying heavily on his feet. He became aware of his ragged breathing, his rapid heartbeat, and the ringing in his ears.

He finally became aware of the absence of pain.

Mostly he became aware of how worried Eden was, despite her flippant question, and how sorry. But she wasn't scared of him. He'd just vamped out in a completely uncontrolled fashion, and she trusted him not to hurt her!

Her trust twisted like a double blade in his heart.

He slowly took his hands away from the dashboard and retracted his claws and fangs.

"Did it work?" he asked her.

"Yeah." She glanced in the rearview mirror. "The Hydra driver's reaction caused a five-car pileup. I hope nobody was hurt."

"At least nobody human." He put back his head and closed his eyes. He desperately needed to rest.

"I left Joe at the apartment," she said as he started to drift off. "Was that okay?"

He didn't like the idea of another hunter at

the safe house, but he wasn't up to complaining about it. "Fine," he mumbled, and drifted off while she drove.

"Hey, Joe, we're home," Eden called as they came in the door. She seemed puzzled when she didn't get an instant response. "Where are you, Joe?"

Laurent rather hoped that this Joe person had left.

She walked into the middle of the living room. "He couldn't have gotten out." Then she smiled. "I bet he's sleeping on one of the beds."

Laurent didn't sense another human, but there was—something.

"I picked up some fresh clothes for you," Eden said, and pointed toward a pile of bags on the floor.

"Thanks," Laurent answered absently. He was impatient to put Eden to work on the laptop, but there was no way he was letting it be hacked into while they had company.

The *something* he sensed was psychic, but the shielded mental impression he got didn't feel vampire. Plenty of the hunters had psychic gifts; this Joe was likely one of them.

Laurent opened the coat closet by the door and tucked the laptop case behind boxes of equipment. It wasn't an ideal hiding place, but it would have to do for now. When he turned around, he glanced at the shopping bags. He was rather touched that Eden had been so thoughtful. Pity the bags were empty.

"I guess Joe must have needed a change of clothes."

She laughed, and glanced up from reading her e-mail. "Right. Just tell me he isn't the type who likes to chew up shoes or anything."

"Not as far as I know."

Her comments piqued his curiosity even more. There was something about this Joe's mental signature that was starting to tickle his memory. Something that reminded him of some of the folk who hung out at the other bar he frequented in Los Angeles. There was a group of loud, boisterous, biker types who came in sometimes, led by a fellow named Shaggy. And he was a—

"Why don't you go check on Joe?"

"I think I will."

Eden's attention was very much on her computer. Laurent was glad of this as he walked down the hall to confront the werewolf lurking in his bedroom.

The male impatiently watching the door was barefoot and wearing what Laurent guessed were *his* new jeans and blue shirt.

"Hello, Joe," Laurent said.

"Hello, Wolf," Joe answered, coming smoothly to his feet.

While they had the same build, Joe was an inch or so taller, a little leaner. His attitude was neutral, but with a strong dose of curiosity.

"I didn't know werefolk worked with the hunters," Laurent said.

"You know damn well we don't," was the reply. Joe got to the point. "Where's Sid?"

So, he'd been caught out at last. Or had he? The werewolf thought his name was Wolf. Laurent decided to bluff. "Right here."

Joe looked him up and down and took a few deep breaths. "You look like a Wolf," he said. "You smell like a Wolf. But you're not Sid Wolf."

"What makes you say that?"

Joe took a step closer, an alpha-to-Prime gesture. "For one thing, Sid's my partner. And more importantly, Sid's a girl."

Sid was a girl? What sort of name was Sid for a female?

"Just checking to make sure you really know her," Laurent lied smoothly. "Why's she called Sid, anyway?"

"It's short for Sidonie," Joe replied, with just a hint of suspicion.

"And you are her—partner?"

"We *work* together."

Laurent didn't miss the slight affront in the werewolf's voice. He held up a hand. "I wasn't suggesting—"

"You better not be."

Werefolk were notoriously touchy about even a hint that they might be fooling around with any species but their own.

"She's my best friend," Joe went on. "Which is why I'm asking you where she is."

"I have no idea," Laurent said truthfully.

"She didn't tell you where she'd be after she turned this case over to you?"

"She's—an independent female."

Or so Laurent gathered from Joe's comments. He didn't know why Clan Wolf would allow one of their precious females out of the house, but if they chose to let their breeding stock roam free, that wasn't his problem. It might actually help him to continue his masquerade for as long as he needed to get Eden to do the work for him.

What he needed right now was to pacify Joe, and somehow hustle the pup out before Eden took any notice.

The werewolf was not at all happy. "She didn't come home this weekend. Her mom's worried. I'm beginning to worry."

"She's a vampire," Laurent pointed out. "Dangerous by nature—even if she is a girl."

"I know you've been passing yourself off as Sid, which isn't such a bad idea—"

"How do you know that? And why isn't it a bad idea?"

"I listened to your girlfriend's taped mission reports, where she keeps referring to you as Sid Wolf. When dealing with humans, disinformation is not a bad thing. Especially when they're hanging out with hunters. But I'd like to know your real name."

"Laurent," he answered without thinking. He cursed himself for not coming up with an instant alias, something that sounded more like a Clan boy moniker.

The shock that surged through Joe sent Laurent back a step.

"*What?*" he demanded.

The werewolf stared at him intently for a few moments, taking long, deep breaths. "Yeah," he said at last. "You're Laurent."

Chapter Seventeen

Eden ran a hand through her short hair. Now that the adrenaline rush from earlier in the evening had worn off, she was pretty much running on empty. But she still had the energy to smile fondly at the memory of Wolf kissing her when he got in the car.

She wanted to call him back to her for another kiss when he went into the bedroom, but made herself stay at the computer. She had to keep distance, perspective.

She managed to concentrate on her e-mail for a while, but eventually the low murmur of conversation from the bedroom caught her attention.

It was several more seconds before she thought, *Conversation?*

Wolf had gone into the bedroom to check on

his pet wolf. Who was he talking to? More importantly, who was talking *back?*

The most logical explanation was that the voices were coming from a radio. But logic really didn't come into the picture when dealing with the supernatural.

Eden got up and walked to the bedroom as silently as she could, then put her ear to the door. She considered it gathering intelligence. One of the voices definitely belonged to her vampire lover. She did not recognize the other male voice, who said:

". . . she keeps referring to you as Sid Wolf. When dealing with humans, disinformation is not a bad thing. Especially when associating with hunters. But I'd like to know your real name."

"Laurent." A pause. *"What?"*

Another pause. "Yeah. You're Laurent."

"What the hell is going on here?"

Laurent whirled to face Eden, who was standing in the doorway, quivering with fury. He wasn't surprised to see her, or at her outrage. Or her question. But he wasn't at all happy with her timing. He was grateful that she didn't seem to be carrying a weapon.

"Not now, sweethear—"

"Who are you?" She was glaring over his shoulder. Then her furious gaze came back to him. "Who are *you?*"

"He's Laurent Wolf," Joe answered for him.

Her attention swung back to Joe. "How did you get in here?"

Hearing himself named Laurent Wolf made Laurent cringe. It made dark things buried deep inside him clamor for his attention, claw to get out. That name didn't belong to him, even though the Clans were matrilineal. He didn't *have* a name. Not even Laurent of the Manticore had ever been officially bestowed on him.

"You let me in," Joe said. "Don't you remember?"

When Laurent noticed the way that Joe was smiling at Eden, the jealousy that jolted through him was as strong as it was unexpected.

"I did no such thing."

Eden was furious, and totally oblivious to the werewolf's attempt at charm. Good.

"I think explanations—and introductions— are in order," Laurent said, trying to grab control of the situation.

"Does your mother know you're here?" Joe asked him.

Laurent's world shattered at that question.

The only thing he was able to grab hold of was the front of Joe's shirt, just before he slammed the werewolf up against the wall.

Joe managed to grab the thumb and little finger of the hand that was choking him and twisted hard.

The vampire could have crushed Joe's throat if he wanted, but he stepped back instead. Joe was left panting and in pain, but at least he could breathe. From the way the Prime had reacted, Joe's guess was that mentioning the prodigal son's mother was a touchy subject.

"Sorry," he ventured.

The woman had moved farther into the room. She was confused, concerned, but mostly she was sending off sparks of anger.

She stepped up to Wolf, and after a second's hesitation, she touched him on the arm. "Wh—"

He turned a glare on her that was pure animal.

Joe tensed, prepared to go to her defense if necessary. But Wolf brushed her hand off and left the room. Vampires could move lightning-fast when they wanted to. Only a moment after Wolf left the bedroom, the apartment door slammed shut. Hard.

Leaving Joe in the awkward position of

being alone with a vampire hunter suffering from a not completely unjustified sense of betrayal.

She turned her outrage on him. "What's this about? And who are you?"

He wished she hadn't gotten back to that. Though she was between him and the exit, he edged closer to the door. "I take it you don't know where Sidonie Wolf is?" he inquired. After all, he was here looking for his partner, not to get involved in the case the vampire and hunter were working. "She's about five-foot-nine, blond, blue-gray eyes. Looks very much like her brother, come to think of it."

She was staring at him so hard, he didn't think she actually heard him.

She took in his bare feet. He saw her recognize the clothes he was wearing. Then her gaze settled on his name pendant.

"Yeah," he said, as she finally came to an unwilling conclusion about what he was.

She took a step back. He didn't sense revulsion, or killing hostility. But she wasn't happy or friendly, either. There were also a lot of weapons in the place, and she was a trained killer. Her kind didn't like his kind any more than they did vampires. Even though she was working with vampires and had mated with Laurent Wolf—

which made her almost family—the revelations of the last few minutes might tempt her to revert to her hunter roots.

"You're extinct!" she said, stunned.

"That's what we want you to think."

She stayed stunned. And he used the edge it gave him to make his own quick exit before she came out of it.

Once out of the apartment, he considered following Laurent. But since he believed the Prime really didn't know where Sid was, he let trailing the lost Wolf go. Laurent might be intriguing, but Sid was priority number one.

Eden didn't know what to do. Other than sit down on the bed, because she couldn't make her legs work. She loved lava, but she didn't like earthquakes. And the last few minutes had shaken her world somewhere around a ten on the Richter scale.

Wolf had lied to her. He'd been lying to her for days, even as they fought together and laughed together and made love.

It shouldn't hurt, but it did. She was being clawed apart from the inside.

Wolf wasn't Wolf. Or not the Wolf she thought he was. Why was this knowledge crushing her?

"Why didn't he tell me?" She spoke into the silence of the room, and almost expected a ghost to step out of the shadows and answer.

What she heard instead was the memory of her aunt's voice.

"They're insidious. And subtle. They don't even notice their own arrogance, because, after all, they are Prime. Prime users. Prime takers."

He'd been mocking her, silently laughing at her because he wasn't who she thought he was. It would have been such a simple thing to correct her mistake when he showed up at the meeting place and she assumed he was the Prime she'd been told would meet her.

"Big joke. Ha. Ha. *Bastard*."

Then she remembered the werewolf saying, *"When dealing with humans, disinformation is not a bad thing. Especially when associating with hunters."*

And now she knew that the supernatural world was even bigger than she'd thought. She'd come face-to-face with a shapeshifter, and what was she supposed to do about it? This revelation—complication—was Wolf's fault as well. She should immediately report the existence of Joe's kind to the other hunters.

But she didn't want to.

That was wrong. Being around Wolf had

changed her, tainted her. She was starting to see things from his point of view, and—

And from his point of view, *she* was the one that needed to be watched out for. The one never to completely trust.

Her ancestors had hunted his ancestors. His had hunted hers. Everybody had long memories.

And that was the way it was always supposed to be.

But here it was, the twenty-first century. Apparently werewolves still walked the earth. Vampires took drugs that helped them blend into the world. They had day jobs. Apparently Clan women had equal rights.

The rules had clearly changed. Why hadn't anybody told the hunters?

It wasn't fair.

She was an anachronism. A joke.

"Oh, woe is me," she muttered.

And why the devil had Wolf stormed out of here before she had the chance to yell at him about his deception? She *needed* to yell at him. Every fiber of her being needed to confront him, and—

She needed to see him, to talk to him. He had been so upset. The look in his eyes had been so—devastated.

Eden's heart hammered hard in her chest, reacting to—Laurent's—pain.

She didn't know how Joe had hurt him, or why, but Laurent Wolf had not been sane when he'd walked out the door.

She fought off an impulse to find him and comfort him, because that was just crazy. But . . . he *was* in a dangerous state. And she *was* a hunter. So it was her duty to find him. *Not* to protect him from himself, but to protect the world from him.

Of course, she had to find him first.

"What did you do, plant a bug on me when I wasn't looking?" Laurent asked the mortal woman who'd silently come up behind him. Not that he'd been unaware of her approach.

"Something like that," Eden answered. "After your last brush with the Manticores, I thought it might be a good idea to keep track of you."

"Gee, thanks."

"Just doing my job."

He wasn't surprised to see that she was carrying a crossbow. She was here to make sure he didn't go blood berserk or ravish maidens, or do whatever vampires did when they had a bad night.

Come to think of it, a little ravishing might be fun. He eyed Eden up and down as a prospective ravishee. Snatching the weapon from her before she could aim it would be easy, but he let it go.

"We have to use technology," she said as the silence became charged. "It's the only way we can compete with all your super senses."

"Wimp. Your ancestors did okay."

"Times change."

Bitterness permeated her words, her feelings, even the way she stood, conveying both alert tension and total defeat.

Somehow—after his blinding red rage and sorrow cleared—he'd expected her to show up, despite all the twists and turns he'd taken. And sure enough, here she was, back in the alley where they'd met. He didn't know how he'd gotten here. Didn't know why. He didn't know why he'd climbed up to the warehouse roof and sat looking at the eastern sky. At first he counted off every second until the sun would rise. But since that was hours away, thoughts eventually began to ramble around his bruised mind.

He'd allowed himself to think about Eden, because those thoughts weren't as painful as the memories clamoring for his attention. After a while, thinking about Eden became a shield against everything else.

He knew she would come to him. He *wanted* her to come to him.

He knew she was going to be pissed, but that was all right.

"I'm not going to apologize," he told her.

She sat down cross-legged beside him, but not too close. "Who's asking you to?"

"Come on. You're thinking, He should have told me."

"That's just ego getting in the way of professionalism. But I've been letting you get past my professionalism from the night we met."

"I haven't been doing it on purpose."

"Ha."

He glanced at her from the corner of his eye. "Maybe a little. I haven't told you a lot of lies," he added.

Though there were also a lot of things he hadn't told her, *big* things—like how he wasn't bound by the Clan rules to protect and serve mortals. Like how he planned to use her to get what he wanted. Like how this op of hers was not his concern.

But that wasn't the same as lying—much— and for some reason, he took comfort in that. Why he should need to take comfort, he didn't know.

"So, Mr. Wolf, you're having trouble with your family, I take it?"

As a way of angling for explanations—and

apology—Laurent thought this was a pretty good opening. The delicate, almost surgical, precision of her tone amused him. And the amusement was almost like a balm.

"Mr. Wolf? Nobody's ever called me that before."

"Everybody has trouble with their family," she went on. "Mine, for example, are dead set against my being friendly with a vampire. *Dead*'s a very operative word when dealing with my family."

"Mine, too."

"Not that we are friends, of course."

He could tell she was remembering the sex; the memory warmed her flesh. And he was drawn to that warmth.

"Not friends," he agreed, and reached over to brush his hand across her cheek and down her throat. "And the word *lover* is—inappropriate."

"Impolitic," she added.

He wanted her. He wanted to throw her on her back and plunge inside her. He wanted to lose himself in the release. He wanted her blood. He wanted her submission. He wanted her cries and pain and pleasure filling his ears and drowning out every other sound and vision drumming inside his head.

"Impolitic, but never impolite." He tried to

sound cool and calm, faintly amused, but his voice was rough with hunger.

Did she hear it? Did she know how close to the edge he was?

He closed his eyes, fighting for control. Though why keep control when he could simply take what he wanted?

But darkness only brought a vision of standing in an elaborately decorated bedroom while Justinian took his pleasure with a moaning, panting blood slave. It had been a show of dominance over the Primes he controlled, nothing to do with pleasure at all. Laurent had been embarrassed and tried to hide it with cynical thoughts.

He wanted to be like Justinian. But he couldn't even figure out how to start.

"Family can really mess you up, you know that?"

"Tell me about it," she commiserated.

"You want to be like them. You don't. You want their approval. You want to escape from them." He sighed. "Humans and monsters alike, we're all the same when it comes to being fucked over by our families."

"Yeah. But we all have to grow up sometime, and make and live with our own choices. Can't blame the folks forever."

"You think so?"

"What *are* we talking about?" she asked at last. "Are we going to get into specifics here?"

"No."

"Fine. Be that way." She rose to her feet. "The sun will be up soon. Want to get back to the safe house before you get a really bad sunburn?"

"I was rather counting on that." He sighed and got up.

"What?"

"I was contemplating having a suicidal impulse."

"Really?"

"No," he responded to her concern. "I was joking." He moved closer to her. Well aware that she was armed and dangerous, he asked, "If I kiss you, will you use that thing on me?"

She finally smiled. "If you *don't* kiss me, I'll use it on you."

Chapter Eighteen

Eden had very little memory of how they'd gotten back to the apartment. She remembered kisses. Long, hard, hot, completely shattering kisses. And his hands on her. All over her, repeatedly bringing her to shaking, screaming orgasms.

And she'd been driving!

Now Wolf kicked the apartment door shut and took her in his arms again. As before, not just his hands and lips and tongue touched her, but sharp teeth grazed across her skin. Pricks of pain sent pleasure rocketing through her and left constantly renewed, aching need in their wake.

He held her tightly, and she clung to his shoulders, too weak from desire to stand on her own. His mouth came down on hers, and she was swept into fire again.

Her hands moved over him, sweeping aside

clothes because flesh *had* to touch flesh. The heat blended them, fused them.

She didn't know when he carried her into his bedroom; she was only vaguely aware of lying on the bed, of his weight as he stretched out on top of her, of pulling him closer.

When she expected a kiss, his wrist covered her mouth. A few drops of warm, sweet liquid touched her tongue, and spread through her. It brought soaring release and an even deeper need for Wolf's touch. *Only* his touch.

He thrust inside her, deep into where he was meant to be. She arched against him, wanting even more. He thrust into her in a hard, fast rhythm while she clutched at his back and his buttocks and ground her hips against his.

When he came, she went with him, drowning in the long, drawn-out moment of pure ecstasy.

When Eden came back to herself, he was lying flat on top of her, heavy and sweaty and boneless.

"You're wrecked," she told him, tugging on his thick braid to move his head so that his chin wasn't poking into her chest.

His answer was a barely audible grunt.

After a long while he slowly lifted his head and looked her in the eyes. "You're the one who wrecked me."

She smiled smugly.

He responded by running his tongue over her nipples. Little aftershocks of pleasure still undulated through her body, yet she wondered—was making love a temporary fix to make him feel better, or an expression of genuine need for her? Or would anybody do? Any body?

Pain fisted in her stomach at that thought, and the kaleidoscope of emotions made her dizzy.

"You," he answered. "At this moment, all I wanted was you."

She realized that he'd read her thoughts. And that the answer had been sweet, but not crystal-clear specific.

She tried not to let it matter. After all, sharing blood didn't make them a couple. They were still practically strangers—she hadn't even known his real name until a few hours ago.

"The sex was great, though."

"Fantastic." He yawned, and mumbled sleepily, "We'll always have Paris, and all that."

She didn't immediately get the reference, and stared at the ceiling while she thought it through.

"*Casablanca*," she finally said. "Rick and Ilsa, and secrets and lies."

"And Nazis. Mustn't forget the Nazis."

"Ilsa was the one who lied to Rick."

"She didn't tell him everything. That's not the same as lying."

"Lies of omission. And I didn't like her. What's with that 'you do the thinking for me' scene? Why couldn't she make up her own mind?"

"She was a woman of her time."

"Bette Davis wouldn't have pulled that 'I won't take responsibility for my own actions' crap."

Laurent lifted his head, and she saw faint outrage in his eyes. She waited for him to defend Ingrid Bergman's honor, but after a moment a smile spread across his face. She couldn't help but grin back.

"How did we get into this conversation?" he asked.

"You said something in the non sequitur line."

He shifted his weight, leaning up on one elbow. "That's not unusual."

She took this opportunity to lever him off her, and sat up. "Breakfast or sleep?" she asked him.

He grasped her wrist and stroked the inside of her elbow. "I've already had breakfast."

Eden looked down and noticed the fading mark of teeth. Vampire bites healed quickly. Soon the mark would be gone, but she knew she'd still feel every place where he'd laid claim to her. Her family would consider them marks of shame.

She wondered if the memories would ever fade. Or if she'd want them to.

Eden slid out of the bed. "Rest, then."

He made a faint sound of protest when she left the room, and Eden got some gratification in knowing that he was reluctant to let her go. But, she assured herself, in the long run, it was better for both of them to be able to let each other go.

"You realize, of course," Daniel said, "that none of this Laurent stuff makes sense."

"No," Joe answered. "I don't."

He'd spent the night trying to pick up Sid's trail with no more luck than he'd had the day before. The whole time he'd been searching, Laurent Wolf's presence in the puzzle had been put on the back burner.

"The important thing is finding Sid," he reminded Daniel.

He almost wished that Daniel Corbett hadn't been pacing the floor in the office when Joe dragged himself in the door. The first thing Joe had done at the sight of Daniel's concerned face was blurt out that he'd come face-to-face with the legendary Laurent. He had not expected a skeptical response from Sid's cousin.

"Shouldn't you be killing a fatted calf or something?" Joe asked.

"Hey, we're not that close cousins. Besides, we don't know for sure if this guy's for real."

Joe tapped the side of his nose. "Oh, yes, we do." There were delicate gradations and variations of scent within a bloodline that showed relationships. Be it human, vampire, or their own kind, werewolves could sniff out kinship bonds. "This Prime is definitely Sid's brother."

"Then why didn't he know where Sid is? Why didn't he care? Why didn't Sid mention him to us?"

All valid and good questions. Which didn't stop Joe from being annoyed at them. "The guy was on the verge of killing me," he admitted. "And walked out before I had time to ask." He touched his throat. "He's got issues. And I've got bruises."

"Over Lady Antonia?"

"Yes."

"Maybe we'd better call her."

"And tell her what? That her oh-so-independent only daughter is still missing? I think I'd rather find Sid than confront her mother."

"Good point."

"And *I'm* not going to be the one to mention Laurent to her. That is not my place. You're her nephew," Joe pointed out.

Daniel held up a hand and counted on his fingers. "Great-, great-, possibly great-nephew. Descended from a brother, and you know that relationships through the female line are more important in Clan culture."

"Coward."

"Yep." Daniel went to Sid's desk. "There's something I've been thinking about trying."

"Wait a minute." Joe looked around. "Cathy's not in yet?"

"She's in," Daniel answered, nodding toward the back of the building. "The full moon came a little early for her this month."

Joe concentrated with his were-senses. Her wolf presence was there, all right. Cathy was locked inside a morphed body and newmade's madness for the next several days. Now another member of the crew was out of the loop, when they were all needed.

"Blast and damn!" Then he looked worriedly at Daniel. "She didn't—"

"Cathy managed to lock herself away in time. No scratches or bites for me. Now, about my idea," Daniel persisted. He picked up the glass paperweight from Sid's desk. "You know this was Sid's mom's, right? Have you noticed how Sid touches it all the time?"

"Yes. And yes. So?"

"You know how Sid and I have been experimenting with techniques for me to be able to read present-day events from objects?"

"I see where this is going, Daniel. You want to try to find Sid by 'reading' the ball." Joe gestured at the object carefully cradled in Daniel's hands. "What are you waiting for?"

Not that Joe thought this would work, but he was willing to try anything. Besides, who was he to discourage his friend from trying to help? There was no doubt that Daniel could pick up accurate energy from the past. Maybe this time . . .

Joe practically held his breath as he watched Daniel close his eyes and concentrate. His fair-complexioned friend grew paler and paler, and he sensed fear, and growing horror. After a few seconds, the paperweight rolled out of Daniel's limp hands and landed heavily on Sid's desk.

"What did you see?" Joe asked anxiously.

Daniel's eyes were open, but he wasn't seeing anything in the office. It took a few moments before he came back to the present and looked at Joe.

"That thing's still too full of Lady Antonia. I

saw the days when—" He shook his head. "I'm not going there. I haven't the right." He took a deep breath. "Nothing about Sid. Sorry." He fell wearily into the desk chair and looked at Joe with bleak eyes. "Now what do we do?"

Good question. Time was a critical factor in a missing-persons case, and Sid had been missing since Friday. He had no leads, not even a sniff of one.

But he did have one anomaly.

"I guess that what I have to do is to accept that your opinion of Laurent's presence in this not making sense makes sense."

"Huh?"

"I'm going to load up on garlic spray, put on some shoes, and go have a talk with him."

Chapter Nineteen

All Laurent had wanted for days was to have Eden and the laptop in the same place at the same time, long enough for her to unencrypt the information that he needed. At the moment he was once again alone in the apartment, wondering why his wishes never seemed to come true.

Maybe if he'd put her to work last night instead of taking her to bed . . .

He smiled at the memory of the pleasure, unable to work up the energy to castigate himself over that lapse in planning.

But he did feel kind of . . . lonely without her being around. Since he'd spent much of his life as a loner and quite liking it, this was disturbing.

He didn't know when he'd decided to keep Eden, but now he knew he would. And he smiled at a decision that should have been alarming.

But—why not Eden? Why not take her with him
when he left town? He was going to start living
the way he'd always wanted. Oh, sure, the fantasy had always included massive orgies with
gaggles of ravishingly beautiful and completely
interchangeable females. But now that sounded
boring. The time when any woman would do
was over. Irrevocably.

"Damn," he murmured, and tried to mind.

But what formed in his head now wasn't fantasy, it was a plan. She'd find the money for
him, then they'd go somewhere exotic to live
happily ever after, having all the sex and room
service they ever wanted.

It ought to be easy. They'd shared enough
blood for him to be able to psychically dominate
her if he wanted to. She'd fight it if he tried, of
course, but a pack Prime was supposed to take
pleasure in the taming. It was the Tribes' way.

It also sounded like a lot of work.

Not that convincing her to stay with him of
her own free will wouldn't be work, but at least
it would be interactive. He liked talking to this
woman. It was a first, and probably a last, but it
was the truth. They weren't Ilsa and Rick, after
all. She wasn't going to let him make up her
mind for her. But he looked forward to getting
started, as soon as she returned.

He'd been dozing when the phone rang earlier. Eden had been in the living room. By the
time he'd gotten out of bed she was already out
the door. Off pursuing bad vampires no doubt.

May she be successful, and hurry home soon.

He became aware of footsteps in the hallway
and recognized the mental signature of the person approaching. It wasn't mortal.

He went to the door and opened it as the
werewolf raised his hand to knock. "What do
you want?"

Joe glanced up and down the hall. "Privacy to
talk," he answered.

Joe could have completely blown his cover
last night; instead he'd said some crazy things.
Things Laurent didn't want to be curious about,
but couldn't help but be.

He stepped back and let Joe inside.

"I waited until your girlfriend left," Joe told
him.

"So we could exchange confidences without
little mortal ears hearing too much," Laurent
guessed. "You should have thought about that
last night."

"I was in a hurry then," Joe said. "I'm not
one for telepathy, and I don't know sign language. I'm sorry she found out things hunters
shouldn't know, especially about my kind, but it

couldn't be helped." He glanced toward the kitchen. "Can I have some coffee?"

"Help yourself."

Laurent sat in the living room and waited for Joe to join him, wondering if he was going to have to kill the werewolf. He could do it quickly and efficiently. Eden might even applaud him for taking out a bad guy.

Killing wasn't his preferred option, but he'd keep the possibility open.

"What are we talking about?" he asked when Joe came out of the kitchen, mug in hand.

Joe leaned against a wall and took a sip of coffee before he looked Laurent in the eye. "Last Friday afternoon Sidonie Wolf took a telephone call from one of the neutral go-betweens that keep the hunters and the clans loosely in contact. Sid was asked to pass information about a Prime hooking up with a hunter, for a reason she did not tell me.

"She did tell me that she was tempted to go to this meeting herself. She said that an experienced private investigator like herself, who dealt with humans on a regular basis and didn't have any personal grudges against the hunters, would be useful on this sort of joint operation.

"I did not think this was a good idea, but I didn't argue with her. I checked up on the meet-

ing and tracked down the hunter who was working with a vampire Prime. I was satisfied that Sid
had passed the info to her clan, and that all was
well. Because of your distinctive Wolf Clan scent
markers, I assumed that you were there for Sid."

"Your nose needs a tune-up," Laurent scoffed.

"Yesterday morning, Sid's mother called to
tell me that Sid didn't come home over the
weekend." Joe's expression became stern, as did
his voice. "Your mother asked me to look for
your sister."

Laurent rose in one furious, fluid move. His
heart raced, and blood red tinted his vision.
"Get out."

Joe didn't move. He didn't break eye contact
or show any sign of fear. Brave, or stupid? Definitely deranged.

After a long, tense silence, Joe said, "You're
clueless, aren't you?"

"I'm Tribe," Laurent said at last. Since he
was going to kill the werewolf, he might as well
admit it. "We don't have *mothers*."

"Antonia would disagree."

"She's dead."

It should not hurt so much to say it.

Joe carefully took a cell phone out of his
pocket and held it out. "I have her on speed
dial, if you'd like to find out differently."

Laurent had knocked the small phone out of Joe's hand before he even noticed that he'd moved. He left a line of blood from his claws across the werewolf's palm, and the sight and scent of it was like a balm.

"Bad joke," he told Joe.

"I take it you don't want to call her right now?"

Laurent turned his back on the werewolf. He didn't know why he was fighting the urge to kill the bastard.

"I'm guessing that I know more about you than you know about yourself."

Laurent whirled back to face the werewolf, barely any control left. "Get out before I kill you."

Joe stood his ground. "Kill me, and you'll never find out the truth."

"I don't want to know the truth."

Joe instantly seized on this. "Ah, ha! You're psychic enough to know that I'm not lying. Sid is your sister. I need you to help find her. How'd you end up working with the hunters instead of her? *Did* she contact you?"

Laurent shrugged. "It was a coincidence. I just ended up where she was supposed to be."

"There are no coincidences in the psychic world. Maybe you heard her call for help?

Blood is thicker than water. You would know that, being what you are."

"A Manticore."

"A Prime of the Wolf Clan."

Laurent couldn't help but laugh. "I don't think so." The devils wouldn't have him; why would he want to sing with the angels?

"Like I said, I know more about you than you do. I know that your sister has spent her entire life looking for you. That's the main reason she works for a missing-persons PI firm," Joe said.

He couldn't have a sister. It wasn't possible. But the werewolf clearly believed he did. "What are you expecting from me, dog meat? I am not interested in this Sidonie female. Or in the hunters' operation."

"Then what *are* you doing here?"

"I'm a Tribe boy; I'm in it for myself. I don't know what happened to your friend, and I don't care."

Yet a voice inside his head was begging, *Ask him, ask him, ask him!* It was the voice of a child, and he told it to shut up.

"Sure, all you care about is yourself."

Joe didn't sound like he believed him. Laurent couldn't imagine where Joe got the notion that he had a nobler side.

"And money," Laurent added. "I care a great deal about having a lot of money."

"You could get a job."

"No, I don't think so."

There weren't a lot of career choices open to his sort. Pimping was traditional among Manticores. Hydras were thugs. Dragons specialized in assassination. Etc., etc., etc. None of the classically criminal enterprises of the Tribes had ever appealed to him.

"You have to have a clue," Joe persisted. "Your presence has to be connected to Sid's being missing. I do not believe it's a coincidence."

"Believe what you want, but stop wasting your time with me," Laurent told the werewolf. "Leave me out of it. I don't care."

"Is that what I'm supposed to tell your mother?"

It was getting harder to keep his fangs and claws sheathed. "It's a pity werewolf blood isn't particularly palatable."

"You're not going to help?"

"I think that's obvious by now."

Joe gave him a disgusted look. The contempt almost boiled off him. "Tribe."

It was a curse, a conclusion. The truth.

What was worse was the flash of pity he read

from the werewolf. Hatred he didn't mind, but he didn't deserve this. He was what life had made him, as Justinian had molded him. He was selfish, lazy, self-serving—a survivor, most of all.

Laurent stood back, crossed his arms, and waited. It didn't take the werewolf long to take the hint. But after Joe was gone, the things he'd said lingered in Laurent's mind.

Your mother asked me to look for your sister.

That, above all else, did not make sense. The two words burned like the lava Eden was so fond of. *Mother. Sister.*

Your sister has spent her entire life looking for you.

Everything went dark around him, thoughts eclipsed by pain. He didn't know how long it was before he realized that his hand covered his eyes. And he didn't know when he'd dropped onto his knees.

How could a few simple words affect him so strongly? They were just words. Stupid *female* words at that. Mother. Sister. Those weren't Tribe concepts. Females were nothing, property to be bought, sold, claimed, traded. They were status symbols at best, and sources of profit.

He'd spent too much time around the Shagal and Reynard Clans lately. The contact must have softened him up to the alien concept of females having importance. And pretending to be a Clan Prime had only made it worse. He'd gotten too far into the act.

And Eden—Eden had taken advantage of his weakened condition. And not even on purpose. Females were insidious that way. But he still wanted Eden. More than anything in the world, he wanted Eden.

Laurent scrubbed his hands across his face and shook his head to clear it. It was better to forget the last hour or so had even happened.

As he got to his feet, he muttered, "Now, where was I?"

Ah, yes, waiting for Eden to come back so he could run off and live happily ever after with her.

Then the memory of fighting a Manticore a few nights ago hit him a fresh blow.

"He offers an exchange of property."

"Justinian has nothing I want."

"He says you will—once you think about the cravings you share."

It had made no sense at the time, and Laurent didn't want it to make sense now. Because if the message meant what he thought . . .

No, Justinian couldn't possibly be that much of a master manipulator. He could *not* be that in control of the situation.

Though Justinian did have a strong streak of prescience. Oh, yes, he could see the future sometimes—or maybe it was more accurate to say that he was very good at arranging it. At least when it came to his own survival.

Laurent had something Justinian wanted; something that would give Laurent his freedom. Justinian couldn't allow that, so he'd taken something Laurent wanted, something—someone—Laurent hadn't even known existed, then made sure Laurent knew about it.

Everything Joe had said was all true—the mother, the sister who'd been hunting for him all her life.

It was all a setup.

"Twist the knife a little more, you bastard."

The question was, what was he going to do about it?

Chapter Twenty

"I quit."

Her cousin Frank gave Eden a confused look. "You mean, after the op is over?"

"No. I mean I quit right now."

They were sitting in her car outside the safe house after spending all day driving around tailing a vampire that was acting "strangely." They'd trailed him in the hopes he'd lead them to his Dawn dealer. No luck there.

He hadn't attacked anyone, hadn't done anything even vaguely aggressive. He'd smiled a lot, mostly while looking up at the clear blue sky. He'd gotten a sunburn. So the only person who'd actually suffered was him.

Watching him, Eden had become more and more agitated. And not at the vampire.

"This is ridiculous, Frankie. Out in the real

world you're a cop—do you see any probable cause for what we're doing?"

"Vampires don't have civil rights, Eden."

"Why not?"

Frank looked out the windshield for a few moments. "They don't pay taxes?"

"I bet they do—at least the Clans and Families."

"Yeah. I guess. Anyway, you can't just quit being a hunter. Not in the middle of an assignment."

"Most hunters have quit. As of right now, I'm one of them. The assignment's stupid."

"People have been attacked!"

"Someone was being chased. No one actually got attacked. Except for me and the Clan guy working with us."

"I thought you said the Hydras have a hit out on you?"

"They won't if I stop interfering with their business."

"So you're running scared."

"Damn right. But that's not why I'm quitting. I believe in honor and duty and all that, but I'm feeling like an idiot and a murderer. Well, not a murderer, exactly, but people—"

"Vampires."

"—are dead because of my actions. I'm not saying that vampires don't need to die sometimes. I no longer think that it's up to me to do it."

"Then who is it up to?"

Frank's outrage did not bother her in the least. "I think the Clans do a pretty good job of policing the Tribes these days." She jerked a thumb toward the building. "Let the Wolf guy handle this. The Clans don't want to lose control of who gets the daylight drugs, Dawn is really their problem."

"Is that what Wolf told you? Is he the one causing you to quit?"

Was Laurent the reason?

Well, the fact that she was out here when she *needed* to be inside with him said something about her reasons.

"Your ride's here," was all she said to Frank as the van pulled up behind the VW.

He reached to open the door. "Just think about it a while longer before you make it official. Please?"

"Ah, come on, don't you want to take over running the op?"

"Hell, no," he answered. "My wife is pissed off enough about my not being home the last few days."

"See how hunting interferes with the important things in life?"

He slammed the door.

Once Frank was gone, Eden parked in the garage and rushed up to the apartment. She felt very little guilt about not telling the other hunters about Joe. Why get everybody all riled up and start another crusade against the werewolves?

"Why don't we all go out gracefully?" she muttered as she opened the apartment door.

"What?" Laurent asked, turning from the computer desk as she came in.

"Thinking out loud about the hunters," she told him. "I see you've finally unpacked the famous laptop," she said, peering past his shoulder.

"Yeah." He sounded downright bitter.

There was a tenseness in the way he stood, and his eyes were hard, but she thought there was dark pain there as well. "What's wrong?"

"Nothing."

"Let me help."

The words were a catalyst for both of them. They met in the center of the room and shared a kiss that was so fierce and desperate it nearly overwhelmed her. She held him as tightly as she could, loving his hard male body, his heat and his scent. Desire rocketed through her as she soared on the way he tasted, the softness of his lips, the sharp danger of his teeth.

She ran her hands down his back and over his buttocks. *Tight little ass*, she thought.

His hand came up under her shirt, rubbing his palm over an already pebbled nipple.

Within moments they were on the floor. Clothes were shed in a frantic rush. They came together in a mating frenzy fueled by desperation.

This could be the last time she felt him inside her, filling her, completing her. The last time she wrapped her arms around the strong, straining muscles of his back, her thighs around his pumping hips. The last hot kiss. The last perfect explosion that sent pleasure beyond pleasure shuddering through her.

It was over too quickly, a bittersweet coupling that left her with an aching satisfaction and longing for more.

He gave her one last, swift kiss. Then he was up, getting dressed, leaving her feeling bereft, almost forgotten. A cold draft from the air-conditioning drifted across her bare, damp skin. It sent a jolt through her, like ghost fingers walking up her skin. Or someone walking across her grave.

His back was to her when she got up. He was looking at his computer. She could tell from the way he stood, neck and shoulder muscles tight, that none of the tension had left him.

It hadn't left her, either.

"What can I do to help?" she asked as she put her clothes back on.

"Nothing."

Though she didn't think either of them were talking about the computer, she asked, "You want me to break into it?"

"No. Not anymore."

He sounded tired, defeated. She didn't get it. "Will you please tell me what's wrong?" She didn't mean to sound quite so testy, but she'd never been fond of mysterious statements.

"The sun has set."

This time she understood what he meant. A fist closed tightly around her heart. "You're leaving."

"Time to move on."

Not just leaving for an evening round of vampire hunting, but leaving for good.

"You're quitting the op," she accused the vampire. "Just like that."

She heard the outrage in her voice and inwardly laughed at her hypocrisy. Hadn't she been about to tell him that she was quitting herself? She was tempted now to suggest they quit together, that they run off together.

She wanted them to run off together.

Maybe they could start a new life together, away from his people and hers. When she'd walked into the apartment she'd been unsure what she wanted of the future, other than to stop being a hunter. Suddenly she knew. She knew in her blood and her bones that she simply wanted to be with him. The revelation sang in her, and hurt her so much she could barely breathe. She didn't know how to begin telling him.

She was going to try to begin, but he turned to look at her and his eyes were blank. His expression was cold, closed. He was everything dangerous and deadly, pale, beautiful as the angel of death. Totally unapproachable.

Wherever the Prime who'd talked to her, laughed with her, made love with her had gone she didn't know, but a statue had taken his place.

But the statue stared at her, caught her gaze, and, for a moment, he drank in her soul. Everything she felt for him poured out of her. He took it in, and gave nothing back. Yet when it was over and he walked out the door, she felt like she'd given him something more precious and sustaining than blood. And that the weak emptiness he left behind was worth it.

This reaction only lasted a moment. Loss remained when she came back to her senses, but she was also completely pissed off.

"You can't walk out on me!" she shouted after him, and spun toward the door.

She fully intended to go after Laurent, but her gaze raked across the desk as she turned. The laptop was gone, but her small cassette recorder sat suggestively next to where Laurent's computer had rested. There was a yellow sticky note on top of it, and she went over to read it.

It read, *Play me.*

"I might be gone by the time you get back," Laurent's voice issued from the speaker. "I suppose I should say something like, *we'll always have Paris.* And I'm leaving you a present. Remember when I interrogated Roswald? I got some information from him that I haven't shared with you yet. If you must hunt down the Dawn makers and their distribution network, there's a Gorgon named Hannibal hiding out in Del Mar you want to eliminate. Have a nice life. And doesn't that sound stupid? Why do people always sound stupid on these things?"

"Good question," she replied as the taped voice ended.

Eden looked around the mostly bare room, overwhelmed to numbness by the sense of utter defeat. Why'd he have to tell her this now, when she was ready to give up? When she *wanted* to give up!

What was she supposed to do now?

She wanted to go home, to her own kitchen and bedroom and *stuff*. She wanted a shower and fresh sheets and to spend the rest of her vacation bemoaning her losses and counting the cost before getting on with her life.

She *had* a life beyond her hunter heritage. Thank God for that. Even if she had to break with her family over her choice, she had other *things* she could do. Even if Laurent Wolf played no part in that life.

Woe is me, and all that.

The point was, she'd been willing to face the pain of her first decision. Now Laurent had left her with another decision to make. He'd thrown the duty and honor stuff right back into her court.

It looked like the Clan Prime was giving her the strength to see the duty and honor thing through to the end, even though he wasn't going to be around to help out.

And why was that?

Maybe because he felt too much for her and *had* to walk away for her own good?

Pathetic. God, she was pathetic.

To alleviate her confused feelings, she put herself back into hero mode. "Do, don't think" was not a bad way to put off coping with emotions.

She listened to Laurent's tape again, and not just for the sound of his voice.

Hannibal of the Gorgons, eh? In Del Mar.

Not a bad bit of real estate. The Tribes had certainly become upscale of late.

Okay, the first thing to do was follow standard procedure and do a scouting run around the area to get a lay of the land. It was best to know the terrain you might have to fight on.

Eden cleaned up and went out for a drive. She'd only gone a few blocks before she noticed the tail.

"Damn."

She could drive like a pro and had a powerful engine under the hood, but the driver behind her was equally good, and driving something more than equal to her VW. She fervently wished she hadn't taken the zapper back into the apartment, because a quick squirt of energy had already proved its usefulness. A cell phone call wouldn't bring her team fast enough at this moment. And a mental cry for help to Laurent wouldn't work, as she wasn't psychic.

On her own, she zigged and zagged around

cars and corners and onto a tree-lined side street, but she was certain she'd been herded into a trap when a pair of vampires dropped from the trees onto the hood and roof of the small car.

She swerved and braked hard in an effort to throw them off, but they clung with all their superhuman strength. She even heard one of them laugh at her efforts. Then a fist came through the windshield. A foot crashed through the window, hitting her hard in the shoulder.

The next swerve was not intentional, and took the car into a tree. There was no airbag in the specialized vehicle. The seat belt not only saved her but slowed her down for a moment too long. The vampires grabbed her and dragged her from the car.

One of them held her arms from behind, the other came up in front of her.

"We meet again," Roswald said, just before the Taser touched her chest.

A hard hand over her mouth stifled her scream.

Chapter Twenty-one

It wasn't—right.

Laurent knew he was deliberately walking into a trap, but that wasn't the kind of wrong his senses were registering. He'd been walking for quite some time, following the telepathic aura that was distinctly Justinian's. The king vampire of the Manticore pack was deliberately keeping his mind open, calling Laurent to him.

After all the trouble he'd gone to to hide his whereabouts from the hated elder Prime, Laurent thoroughly resented Justinian's mental energy shining out like a beacon calling him home.

It was a game to Justinian. All of Laurent's life had been a game for Justinian's pleasure.

Laurent stopped to pull himself together. There was a bench nearby under a palm tree. He took a seat to think.

He was no child. He was turning himself in to

Justinian of his own free will. This time he had
actually chosen to play the game.

His choice. It would be important to remember that in the hours and nights to come.

He took a deep breath and caught the scent
of salt air moving on a faint western breeze. The
touch of the air held the familiarity of Antonia's
caress on his cheek.

That Antonia was alive, that she had a
daughter, still stunned him. All his questions
pressed like a crushing weight on him.

Maybe he didn't need to know.

He'd never met this sister; he could leave her
to her fate. The only person who would think
less of him was himself. And Eden if she ever
found out.

She was good for him. So good that the effect
was devastatingly bad for his survival instinct.

To escape from all the junk filling his head
Laurent made himself look around. It wasn't
just the breeze that was familiar. The houses lin-
ing the street were old, many with the carefully
tended grass lawns that were so bad for the
city's desert environment. But real grass had
been a popular status symbol here since—

When?

*Belisarius pushed his face into the earth. The
older, bigger cub's knee pressed hard against his*

spine. The grass was sharp and spiky, wet from being recently watered. The fresh aromas of earth, water, and growing things did not make up for the pain and humiliation of having been caught outside the house again.

Laurent stood up and turned slowly, taking everything in with all his senses—sharp vampire sight, hearing, smell, and the all-important psychic awareness. Echoes assaulted him, from a past mostly forgotten.

He knew this place.

And now he knew what wasn't right; the neighborhood looked all wrong. Everything seemed so much smaller, so much older. Of course, it wasn't so much that the neighborhood had shrunk, he'd just gotten a lot taller.

Laurent's lips lifted in a semblance of a smile, and he shook his head. He'd been to San Diego before as an adult, but this was the first time he realized that it was the place where he'd spent a good part of his childhood. Well, he'd spent a lot of time deliberately repressing memories. He couldn't blame himself for having been successful.

He shifted the computer case from one hand to the other, and squared his shoulders. He didn't need Justinian's beacon call anymore; he knew exactly which house to walk up to. He pushed all the memories bubbling up firmly back down as he did so.

There were guards placed around the perimeter of the property, but no one approached Laurent as he walked up to the door. He didn't bother to knock, but the door was opened for him.

"Hey, Igor," Laurent said to Justinian's human slave. "Long time no see."

"It's been two weeks," the man answered. "And don't call me Igor."

A proper Tribe Prime would cuff the mortal for showing such disrespect. "Guess I know where I am in the pecking order," was Laurent's response.

"You're keeping him waiting." The slave turned and walked away.

Laurent followed down a long hall, and up a staircase, fighting dread with each step. "The place hasn't changed much, has it?" he commented, but got no answer.

Then again, the mortal hadn't been born the last time Laurent was in this house. Haunted house, he thought. He'd never encountered any real ghosts, but who needed them when memory served?

Before he could get any more morbid, they reached an open door at the top of the stairs. It looked like Justinian had moved back into his old bedroom. The slave held out a hand for the case, but Laurent ignored him and walked inside. He already knew that Justinian was alone in the room. He hadn't expected Justinian to look so much older. As Igor had pointed out, it had only been a couple of weeks.

"Belisarius is dead," Justinian said, as though in explanation. "You're all I have left."

That was *not* the greeting Laurent had expected.

Laurent put the laptop case on the floor and shoved it across the tile floor with his foot. "This is what you want."

Justinian was seated in a chair next to an unlit stone fireplace. The furniture was Stickley, but the arrogant attitude of the Manticore Prime made it seem like a throne.

"Thank you for returning the Tribe's property," he said.

"Not *your* property?"

"Manticore is mine."

Laurent wasn't going to argue with him, he didn't care.

"You came for the female," Justinian said after silence dragged on for a while. "I knew you'd want a Wolf bitch. It's in your blood." He smiled, his eyes full of dark memories. "In our blood."

Laurent had never really wanted to kill him before now. He rubbed his tongue over emerging fangs, but kept the sharp points from showing.

"She was found almost by accident," Justinian went on. "Roaming the streets as though she had a right. And I thought, Laurent would like a pet. I knew I could use her to lure you back home—though it took you long enough to understand my message. Perhaps you were having too much fun toying with the mortal bitch."

"Home?" This time Laurent could not keep his contempt in check. He had no intention of discussing Eden, who was thankfully safely out of this.

"You know I've never wanted you anywhere but at my side. But since I've given you a few decades to see the world, it's time I called you back. You were eager enough to answer the call a few weeks ago."

"I was eager for the fortune you promised me."

"That isn't the true reason you came at my call. You crave my approval."

"I—"

Laurent wouldn't let himself go on. Raving and ranting was no way to confront Justinian about the past. The way to survive was to figure out the game, and either play, or figure out a way to avoid playing. He hadn't figured out this game yet. Justinian was acting like he was welcoming home a prodigal son. Was the old boy pretending to be feeling his years? For vampires were mortal, despite their long, long life spans. Was the scam to feign a sudden need for reconciliation to somehow gain Laurent's loyalty?

"Home?" Laurent repeated. "You've never acknowledged me, so how can your lair be my home?"

Justinian laughed, and looked very pleased with himself. "I'm granting you mating privileges, exclusive rights. That's a start."

Primes could have as many mortal females as they pleased, but usually only the king of the lair had rights to one of their own kind. Rights he shared sparingly with his favored offspring.

Laurent let out a long, low whistle. "That is a generous gift," he acknowledged. And this was no time to argue or show suspicion. "Show me the female."

"On one condition."

Laurent sneered. "Of course. It can't be anything so simple as trading a female for the Patron's wealth, can it?"

"Belisarius is dead."

"We were both there when he died," Laurent pointed out. "He lost the fight with the Reynard Clan Prime. If you're going to ask me to avenge his death, we both know you can forget it. No love lost between Belisarius and me. And it was a fair combat over the Clan brat's bondmate."

Justinian nodded solemnly. "A fair fight," he agreed. "But I still lost my heir. I lost my second in command. I lost the acknowledged continuance of my bloodline. You are all I have left."

He didn't sound any more pleased about this than Laurent felt, but the older Prime did sound—weary. Maybe a little desperate and lost. Justinian was a traditionalist. His stubborn strength of will was the reason the Manticores remained mired in all the ancient, dark ways of the Tribes.

"Are you saying you want me as your heir?"

"You are all I have left."

"So you've said." Laurent felt as if a cold bucket of slime had just been poured over him.

Once upon a time, he would have felt gleeful joy at such acknowledgment from Justinian—if only for the chance of sticking his tongue out at Belisarius. Then the moment would have passed, and he'd have turned Justinian down cold. Lead a Tribe pack? No way in hell.

But right now was not the time to say no. He didn't quite believe Justinian, anyway. The old boy was a master at holding out a carrot, then beating him with a stick.

"You are my son," Justinian said. He said it through gritted teeth.

The words simply left Laurent empty. He glanced around the bedroom. "I don't see any witnesses."

"Tomorrow night," Justinian promised. "I will call you son before all the household."

"Fine." He was here on business. "I want the female now."

Justinian seemed relieved to accept this as capitulation. "You'll be taken to her," he said, and called for his slave.

He was taken to the room full of windows. Laurent recognized it with a painful twist of memory as he caught sight of the beautiful young woman seated on the bed. He was very glad that she wasn't naked.

She looked too much like Antonia, though her blond hair was short. And she was bound with the same silver manacles he remembered circling his mother's wrists.

She looked him over coolly, exhibiting not a bit of fear. He stood frozen as the door closed behind him, and her gaze traveled slowly from his feet to his face, until their gazes met and held. Her eyes were the exact shade of blue-gray as his own.

"Laurent," she finally said. "It's about bloody time."

"You look like Antonia." He knew he sounded like a child.

She smiled. "So do you."

He shook his head. "I have a sister. How could I have a sister?"

"I'm Sid, by the way."

She sounded calm, but he could feel that she was anxious, as afraid of this going badly as he was.

"I know. I've been Sid myself."

Beautifully sculpted brows lowered over her familiar eyes. "What?"

"A long story. Something of a farce, really. With werewolves."

"So you've met Joe. I hoped you would, when I let them kidnap me."

While this comment was puzzling, Laurent wasn't ready to talk about the last few days. He came closer to the bed.

"How is this possible? How are *you* possible?" His voice was tight with pain.

"Our mother was rescued. I'll let her tell you her story. But the problem with being rescued by her protective Clan was that she ended up in another sort of prison for years. She wanted to march out and find you; instead she was sheltered and counseled and kept in the Clan citadel for her own good. She did need to be loved and cherished, but she was stronger than they would believe. She eventually formed a relationship with a Corvus Prime, and I was the result.

"Now, I have a question for you." Her expression turned stern. "I want to know whether all the time and effort I've gone to, looking for you, was worth it. Are you a Tribe or a Clan boy?"

Laurent shrugged. "I'm Prime," he answered. "That's the only thing I'm really sure of."

"That's not encouraging."

"It's all I've got for you at the moment. It's been a rough week."

She lifted her manacled wrists. "Tell me about it."

Laurent smiled. It seemed his sister shared his sense of humor.

He had a sister. Whoa.

He hoped this bittersweet pleasure wouldn't fade.

She studied him carefully. "You're thinking that the old bastard could convince you to take a tribal view of the matter."

"It's happened before." He looked at his

watch. But he knew when the sun would come up, and how then the room would be full of light. "I'm supposed to be raping you right now."

She bared fangs at him. "You could try."

"Nah. I've already got a girlfriend," he answered. Though Eden was well out of this, he missed her. "If she saw me here, now, she wouldn't agree about the girlfriend description."

"Girlfriend. Now, isn't that an odd term for a Tribe boy to use?"

"I have a lot of identity issues."

He finally managed to walk up to the bed, but he could not bring himself to even sit down on it.

"I—Antonia—" Laurent cleared his throat. "She used to be kept in here."

"So the bastard gleefully informed me." Sid lifted her manacled hands to grasp his fingers. Her touch felt like Antonia's, as well. "He's trying to use your identity issues against you. Controlling you is essential to his game plan."

Laurent cocked an eyebrow at his newfound sibling. "Aren't you doing the same thing? Didn't you mention something about *letting* yourself be captured?"

She lifted an eyebrow back. "I acted on intuition. Also, I was way outnumbered when the fight started." She laughed. "From all the yelling around here the last few days, I believe that you and—your girlfriend's a hunter?—have reduced the Manticore population. And this knockoff drug they take isn't helping their cause any."

"They have a supply of Dawn?"

"Laurent—" She reacted sternly to his enthusiasm. "You do not want to start taking that shit."

"Easy for you to condemn. When the sunlight comes through those windows, you can just work on your tan."

"I'm not condemning; I'm saying that Dawn isn't safe. Justinian's boys are getting twitchy. He doesn't want them taking it, but he can't stop them." She squeezed his hands. "That's one of the reasons he wants you back. You're going to lead his tribe into the future."

Laurent stepped back. "I'm no leader. No alpha Prime." Which was the last thing a Prime would normally confess to. He gave Sid an ironic smile. "I be a lover not a fighter, sister mine. So you might not want to count on me to come to the rescue."

"You're here," she answered. "I'll count on you being cunning and resourceful."

He didn't feel like he was either. After all, he was here, precisely where Justinian wanted him to be. He'd given up his one bargaining chip. His sister was in chains. He wasn't completely certain Justinian couldn't talk him into anything he wanted. The Dawn was tempting.

Nobody was safe, or saved.

Still, he said, "I'll think of something."

Sid glanced out one of the many windows. "It's going to be dawn soon."

Laurent backed toward the door. "You'll be all right? Nobody's going to come in and—"

"Justinian won't let them lay a finger on me. He still has that much control of his pack. I'm supposed to be your private sex slave."

These words wouldn't have turned the stomach of a proper Tribe Prime. Incest wasn't really an issue for them.

He turned away from his sister, but waved a hand before reaching for the doorknob. "I'll—be back later."

Out in the hall, with the closed door between them, Laurent leaned his head against the wood, lost about what to do next. It was so much easier to be one of the bad guys. Maybe he should just go with that.

Then a commotion at the front of the house drew his attention, and a familiar mortal presence registered itself on his senses.

Eden Faveau might not be psychic, but she

made a very strong impression. Especially when she was shouting at the top of her lungs.

"*Shit.*" Now the one person he thought was safe was here. He smashed a fist angrily into the wall.

Then he raced toward the front room to see just how much trouble Eden was in now.

Chapter Twenty-two

"Touch me there again, and I'll kill you," Eden warned the Prime she'd managed to kick in the balls.

He'd been too busy fondling her to consider that she might be able to defend herself. Maybe he didn't think she'd recovered from the Taser shocks, or maybe he didn't think women could fight. But he'd just learned a lesson.

He surged up off the floor with his fangs and claws extended. A second vampire grabbed her from behind and held her still while the first Prime stalked toward her.

"I'm going to slash your face, first." He touched his sharp claw points to her cheeks, then pulled his hands back so she could get a good look at them. "Scared?"

"Of course she's scared," a familiar voice drawled.

Eden managed to turn enough in her captor's grip to watch Laurent move into the room with a dangerous fluid grace. The effect was rather like a cheetah loping into a room full of pussy-cats.

She barely recognized him.

"Melodrama." Laurent sighed.

Then he grabbed her by the hair and pulled her out of the other Prime's hold. He forced her head back with casual ease, twisting his fingers in her hair. "You don't need to ask permission to terrify someone. Just *do* it." He leaned close to whisper in her ear. "Fight me, and it will really hurt."

Though the body pressing hard against her back was familiar, she barely recognized his voice. Her neck ached and her scalp burned from the pressure.

He spoke over her head. "If you touch her again, Alexos, I'll be the one to kill you."

"Of course he will," a new voice said.

Laurent let go of her head but kept an arm around her waist, tight as a steel band. She glanced toward the newcomer and felt jarring fear as she recognized the Prime from an old photo in his dossier.

"Justinian."

His gaze barely flicked her way when she

spoke his name. He concentrated his attention on Laurent, and he smiled. Eden couldn't fathom what that meant. Why was Laurent here?

Justinian came to stand in front of Laurent and gave him a nod of approval.

The monster was older than in the surveillance picture, but the debauched angel beauty was still there. The photo only hinted at the coldness and arrogant contempt that permeated this creature's being, though.

"Did the hunter follow me here?" Laurent asked.

"Oh, no," Justinian said. "I sent for her."

The steel band around her waist tightened further, bringing a gasp of pain from her. Laurent knew she was hurting, but he didn't ease up. She was tempted to struggle, but something about Laurent's dangerous tension as he faced Justinian warned her to keep quiet.

"Why?" Laurent asked.

"Another present."

"You are being far too generous." There was nothing polite in Laurent's tone.

"Very likely," Justinian answered.

He was smiling, sounding pleasant, but Eden recognized the implied threat in every word.

She glanced at the four other Primes who were hanging back, watching and waiting. They looked mean, and they looked greedy. Or maybe hungry was a better term—hungry for violence, hungry for power. Hungry for her, she realized as she noticed the way they darted heated glances at her. It made her skin crawl.

A couple of them didn't look very healthy, either; they were more pasty than pale. Dawn users, she guessed.

"I was surprised you didn't bring her with you," Justinian continued.

This drew Eden's attention away from the rest of the audience. She could barely breathe as it was, but she held her breath, waiting for Laurent's response.

"You were offering me something better," Laurent said. She felt his shrug all along her body. "No reason I can't have them both."

"A harem is a Prime's right," Justinian agreed. "But I was thinking about the female's other use. You did acquire her to unlock the secrets in the Patron's computer, didn't you?"

"Acquire?" Eden was too outraged to keep quiet this time.

Laurent's free hand came across her mouth, effectively silencing her. He had complete control of her. And it was growing clearer by the second that Laurent was just as ruthless and evil as the other Primes gathered around her like carrion feeders. She was dizzy with fear, confusion—and growing revulsion.

"I thought you might have your own expert," Laurent said.

The older Prime laughed. "Nonsense. As usual, you were trying to thwart me." He put an elegant hand on Laurent's shoulder. "From now on we won't play those sort of games, my son."

Son?

Eden felt ready to faint.

The shock from the other vampires jerked her back into the present.

"Son?" one of them demanded. "He's been running with the hunters slaughtering us!"

Justinian swiftly turned and raked claws across the younger Prime's face. "With my permission!" A deep snarl rumbled from his throat, and everybody backed away. He glared for a couple of seconds, then nodded as gazes dropped. Justinian turned back to Laurent. "You see what I have to put up with?"

"They're a handful, all right," Laurent answered. "Do you want to use my blood slave's computer skills now?"

"Take the day with her," Justinian said magnanimously. "You know I do my business at night."

Eden was overwhelmed by the news that Laurent was a Tribe Prime. Even worse, he was Justinian's son.

She wanted his hands off her. She wanted to spit in his face. Most importantly, she wanted to kill him.

Instead he dragged her along behind him like a rag doll, up a flight of stairs and into a heavily curtained bedroom. He kicked the door closed, tossed her onto her back on a wide bed, then turned on a dim overhead light.

"Well, isn't this another fine mess you've gotten me into," he said, looking down at her with his hands on his hips.

"You scum-sucking maggot bastard!" was her reply.

"I'm a bastard, all right. But if you call me a son of a bitch I'll be tempted to hurt you."

"You're Tribe. Manticore!"

"Yep." The succinct word was not spoken with any relish.

Eden noticed that her cheeks were wet; she was crying in front of a lying Tribe bastard. This only made the anger and humiliation worse. "I slept with you!"

"And you're likely to be sleeping with me again." The way he looked her over reminded Eden that she was lying on the bed like some barbarian's war prize.

And he'd called her a blood slave.

It was said that blood slaves were completely addicted to their Tribe masters. She and Laurent had shared blood. She'd thought it was a mutual gift—of trust, of pleasure. But he must have been doing it simply to use her. How much did it take to turn someone into a helpless addict?

She'd been so naive. Stupid. Gullible. All those years of training had been forgotten almost from the moment she met him.

All because he was so damn beautiful, so challenging, so charming—so good in bed.

She sat up, her head and stomach reeling. "I think I'm going to be sick."

He crossed his arms. "Well, that certainly feeds my ego."

"I was an idiot to trust you."

"Not exactly an idiot. I'm a very accomplished liar. Perhaps *liar* isn't the right word. Actor. You saw what you wanted to see, Eden. I went along with you. We even kicked some Tribe butt. Now, didn't that make you happy?"

"Not as happy as it will make me when I kill you."

He smiled. Then the smile turned into a long, deep laugh.

"It's not an empty threat," she pointed out.

He stopped laughing, but there was still amusement in his eyes, where before they'd been hard and angry. "I love a woman who talks like that," he told her. "It must be genetic." He looked surprised for a moment, and added. "In fact—"

He made a strangled sound and turned his back on her. He muttered something she couldn't make out.

"In fact, what?" she demanded.

"You don't want to hear it." He faced her again. "You won't believe me."

"What the hell are you talking about?"

"Love," he answered. "*I* don't want to believe it. I've never been so scared in my life, but I have to say it. I love you, Eden Faveau."

"You're saying that to hurt me."

"I love you," he repeated. "There's nothing I can do about it, nothing I want to do about it—except prove it to you. But discovering it right now is damned inconvenient for both of us."

Whatever it was he meant by love, she did not want to know. "Liar. Scheming rat bastard liar."

He shrugged.

It annoyed her that even though he'd revealed his true identity, Laurent was still acting like—Laurent. Downstairs in front of the other Primes he'd been all macho and nasty, but once they were alone, he'd reverted to the Laurent she'd thought she'd known for the last several days.

The Laurent she'd been so attracted to.

"Did you put a glamour on me?" she demanded.

"A what?"

"You know, did you use your telepathic powers to make me attracted to you?"

"You wish. Then you wouldn't have to take responsibility for your actions. The blood we shared wasn't what drew you to me." He shook a finger at her. "The seduction was mutual. Have I forced anything on you?"

"Not that I remember."

"Eden."

"Okay," she admitted grudgingly. "No."

"You wanted me because you wanted me." He gave an unabashed happy grin. "Thank you. I'm not used to being wanted for myself."

He sounded too honest, too vulnerable. This touched her, though he had to be playing her. "Oh, please," she countered. "What's not to want?"

"I know. I'm perfect. But I generally don't get to know my partners or let them know me. You're my first."

Eden couldn't stop her raucous, bitter laugh. She got to her feet. "Excuse me, but how do I know *you*? First you let me think you're Sid Wolf. Then the werewolf calls you Laurent Wolf. Now I find out you're actually a Manticore." She shuddered, and couldn't stop the grimace. She'd had sex—lots of really good sex—with a Manticore. "How did you convince a werewolf's legendary senses that you're a Wolf Clan vampire? Or was the werewolf in on a scheme to con me?"

"Werewolves are honest, loyal, and true. Shame on you for thinking one would do anything but bite a Manticore on the ankle if they got the chance. Joe just wanted me to help him find—someone for him."

"The real Sid Wolf."

"Yeah." His voice was tight, and his expression had gone blank.

"But why did he ask you for help? Why did he mistake you for a Wolf?"

Eden wanted desperately to know, to really know, Laurent. If only to learn how she'd gone so very wrong in coming to care for him.

He didn't answer her immediately, and she saw a sadness and fear in his eyes that couldn't be an act.

Ridiculously, foolishly, she wanted to throw her arms around him. But she didn't move; she waited for him to make up his mind. About what? Whether or not to trust her? She was his prisoner; he owed her nothing. And yet . . .

He'd said he loved her.

"Love means trust," she said.

Laurent cleared his throat, twice, and took a long, deep breath. "My mother," he said. "Was . . . is Wolf Clan."

Eden suddenly, vividly, recalled a conversation they'd had in her car. He'd asked her to tell him all she knew about Justinian.

"You do know that he started a war between the Manticores and local clans, including yours back in the 1880s? In fact, it was over his stealing a female from the Wolf Clan, wasn't it? We hunters don't know many of the details even if we did help run the Tribes out of town. Did you ever get her back?"

He had gone very still. Once again he was staring out the windshield, and his expression was blank. "No."

For all that his answer was brusque and cold it made her aware that in some way he was hurting and vulnerable. It occurred to Eden that Sid Wolf was likely related to the kidnapped Wolf female. What was somebody else's ancient history for her might be a recent tragedy for the long-lived Clan.

"Did you know her?"

"Your mother," she said now. "She's the Wolf Justinian took. Oh, God, I'm sorry, I—"

He held up a hand to silence her. And gave

one of his fatalistic shrugs. "How is it so many people know more about my history than I do?"

She hesitated for a moment, then replied, "I don't. The hunters don't know about what happened to—your mother."

She'd almost said *Clan female* in the depersonalizing way she'd been trained to think about vampires. If there was one thing Laurent whateverhecalledhimself had taught her, it was that vampires were people, too. Whatever other deceptions he practiced on her, she couldn't see vampires as just soulless monsters anymore.

"Not that some of us don't still need killing." He picked up on her thoughts.

"You said your mother is Wolf Clan? Is she all right? Does Justinian still—"

"He sold her a long time ago."

Eden was repulsed by this answer, but she was not surprised.

"I thought she was dead," Laurent went on. "I spent years looking for her." He gave a soft, bitter laugh. "Justinian never understood why I was always running away. Until I heard she died in a fire. I didn't think there was any more reason to search for her then. I guess I was wrong. We're telepaths," he went on. "I don't understand why she didn't—" He shook his head. "Never mind."

"Maybe she couldn't," Eden said.

She hated the way Laurent stood there, as both a heartbroken child and a confused, embittered adult. She couldn't believe that this was some sort of ploy, no matter how good an actor he claimed to be. She couldn't help but try to help.

"Maybe she was hurt in this fire. Maybe she suffered post-traumatic stress from what was done to her and her psychic powers don't work anymore. Are you even sure she's still alive?"

"Joe tells me he has her number on speed dial. And—there's other evidence."

"What?"

"Her daughter. Her name's Sid." He shook his head, looking thoroughly disgusted. "Why do I always tell you too much?"

Eden could have easily disputed this statement, but instead she said, "Sid's your *sister?*" She threw up her hands in frustration. "Why did you pretend to be her? What's with the computer? Where do I come into this? Why did you leave?" She cringed. "I didn't mean to ask that." The answer to her last question was deeply important to her, even though she hadn't known she was thinking it until she blurted it out.

"I'm an opportunist. It's a healthy survival trait, so I don't apologize."

"You used me from the first."

"I did help with your investigation, now didn't I? I had your back in all those fights."

All true, she admitted. But there was a sting in it, wasn't there? "Why?"

"You know, you are my prisoner. I don't have to explain myself to you."

He was infuriating, but Laurent made her laugh. "Oh, come on, there's nothing worse than a pouting villain. Explain your evil plan to me. Gloat a little. A Tribe prince needs the practice," she added.

Her words seemed to hurt him, and she almost apologized. Then she remembered that she was a prisoner. She wanted to suspect that Laurent hadn't deliberately gotten her into this mess, but he had gotten her into it. She didn't owe him apologies. But that urge to comfort him . . .

Damn.

She didn't think she was going to be able to get rid of it. She ached for him. She cared for him. It made no sense, but she wasn't going to try to deny it.

"You've messed me up, you, you, Wolf/Manticore hybrid."

"The feeling is mutual, Faveau. I mean, getting involved with a hunter? That's just wrong."

She noticed that they were standing near each other, and had no idea how it had happened. When they'd started this heated conversation, the width of the room had been between them.

He was wearing a black shirt, with the cuffs turned up, and she noticed something about his wrists that she hadn't before. His arms were long, elegantly muscled, his hands long-fingered, his wrists graceful. And the pale skin on the inside of them was completely blank.

"No tattoo," she realized.

"No tattoo," he affirmed. He pointed a finger at her. "You should have noticed sooner. Especially with all the times you've seen me naked."

She slapped the flat of her palm against her forehead. "I am such an idiot!"

All Clan Primes, or at least the ones who claimed to serve and protect humankind, wore a tattoo of their clan's heraldic symbol on their wrist. In Laurent's case it should be a wolf's head. It was the first thing she should have asked to see.

Not that his taking advantage of her was her own fault, but she should have been more observant.

"Never mind seeing you naked," she said. "Why did you hang around? Why did you help me?"

"At first I was just looking for a place to hide."

"Justinian was after you?"

"Not for the first time. And I had something he wanted."

"The computer."

"Which might very well hold information about the Dawn drug. I didn't lie to you about that. I don't know for sure, but it seems likely that Garrison was involved in its development."

"So helping me seemed like a fair trade for shelter?" He nodded. "What else is on the laptop? Let me guess: something you needed a hacker's help to access. When you found out about my day job, you decided to hang around to persuade me to break into the system."

"Precisely."

Yet for some reason he had decided to turn the laptop over to Justinian. It wasn't his fault she'd gotten captured. He *had* tried to keep her out of it when he walked out. He'd told her he didn't need her expertise.

Why?

The answer was easy to guess: Sid.

Aw.

"Why are you smiling at me like that, Faveau?"

"You traded the computer for your captured sister."

He grimaced. "It sounds so—"

"Heroic."

"—stupid when you put it like that."

"It's not stupid. You were trying to do a good thing."

He sighed. "Yeah. Trying. When I try to do good things, they generally turn out stupid. I'm not a hero, but every now and then I get this—impulse. It's got to be the Wolf genetics working to mess me up. I'm no good at being good." He wiped a hand wearily across his face. "And I'm too lazy to make a good bad guy. And I'm tired. Can we stop fighting for a while?" he asked. "I could really use a good day's sleep."

She was pretty tired herself. And bruised. And she supposed the headache she'd tried valiantly to ignore was aftershock from her forehead banging into the steering wheel of her car. And then there'd been the Taser. And all the stormy emotional mess.

"I'm still angry with you," she told him. "But I guess we can pick it up later."

Laurent moved closer to her. She should have tried to step away when he took her in his arms, but she found comfort in his embrace. She found strength and reassurance, and felt his need for the same. Maybe it was a lie, a lie they told themselves if not each other, but being in his arms felt right.

"Later," he whispered in her ear.

Then he carried her to the bed and wrapped his body protectively around hers.

Chapter Twenty-three

"There have got to be vampires involved in this," Joe said to Daniel. "I wouldn't have so much trouble tracking otherwise, if there weren't vampires involved. Their psychic energy cancels out mine, and messes up my nose—at least in large groups. I've been to enough vampire parties and come home feeling like I had a full sensory head cold," he went on. "Sid must have run afoul of the druggie Tribe guys that are in town."

"My guess is that you've figured that from the first, but didn't want to think about it."

He and Daniel were in the office. Joe was sitting with his feet up on his desk, a mug of coffee cradled in his hands, and he was really, really tired. And the exhaustion was nothing in comparison to the dread growing in him. He had to find a way to help his best friend, and soon.

Before the hell that had happened to her mother began to happen to her.

"It's too bad I couldn't get Laurent to be of some use," Joe muttered angrily. "Jerk."

Daniel was seated at Sid's desk, his gaze on her glass paperweight. He looked up. He wasn't any more rested than Joe. "There are other vampires we can call," he reminded Joe. "Good vampires—to fight the bad ones."

"I know. I've been avoiding thinking about that, too. It's the last thing Sid would want."

Daniel gave a tense nod. "I don't like to think about her Clan's reaction, either. But isn't it better for her to be a prisoner of people who love her?"

Sidonie Wolf was the hardest thing for a vampire female to be. She was free. This was the twenty-first century, and more and more of the young females were demanding changes to the sheltered, restricted, pampered way Clan women had always lived. This change had started back in the 1960s, but the movement was building up steam now.

Some females were going out to live on their own for years at a time until their matris called them back home. Sid was the first who'd openly declared that if her matri called, she'd only return home to mate if she wanted to. The Primes, the Matri, and the elders were uncomfortable at best with these changes. Some saw Sid as a rebel. Many were downright hostile. And Sidonie Wolf blithely ignored them and lived on her own, worked at a dangerous profession, and had always insisted that she was free to do anything any other American woman could. She was a source of major controversy among her kind.

There were plenty of vampires who would love to see her get in trouble, to need rescuing. And there'd be a terrible price for her to pay for it. Joe hated the thought of seeing his friend's wings clipped, to see her only allowed out surrounded by a band of smug Prime bodyguards.

So he still hesitated in making a call to Wolf Clan for assistance.

All in all, it was much easier to be of the werefolk than of vampire kind. While they had plenty of problems within and without their culture, at least gender equality wasn't something they had trouble with.

Joe drained his coffee. "I'm thinking too much. I need an action plan." He watched as Daniel delicately lowered a finger to touch the paperweight, then grimaced. "What are you doing?"

Daniel slowly retracted his touch from the glass and focused his gaze on Joe, while rubbing his finger as though it ached. "I think Justinian is involved in this."

"Daniel, you see into the past," Joe reminded his seer friend.

"I have been seeing into the past with the glass ball," Daniel answered. "The strongest impression I've been getting from it is of a house. A house here in town, I'm sure of that. I keep seeing it over and over."

"The house where Lady Antonia was held," Joe said. "The paperweight was hers—"

"Justinian's house," Daniel interrupted. "I believe that is where he's holding Sid. I can't explain all the impressions I'm getting—it's sort of like in the past, but with shadows from the present sort of smoking up the vision."

Joe thought about it for a while. "If Justinian came back to his old lair—" He nodded. "Maybe you are picking up on Sid. I sure as hell hope so. It's a start. A place to look. Do you think you could find—"

"You could ask Lady Antonia," Lady Antonia said from the doorway.

Both men stood as the tall woman who looked so much like a slightly older version of Sid closed the office door and came up to Joe's desk.

"Neither of you noticed me come in," she

said. "I'm not sure if that's a sign I might finally be getting some of my psychic powers back, or if the two of you are too distracted for your own good. It's probably the latter."

"How'd you get here?" Joe blurted out. He'd never seen her anywhere but inside the safe confines of Clan Wolf's La Jolla compound.

"I borrowed a car," she answered. "Sid taught me to drive." She waved for them to sit back down. "I've heard most of what you said, so there's no need to fill me in."

She took the seat next to Joe's desk while he remained on his feet, unsure what to do or say. There was something about Antonia, head of House Antonia of Clan Wolf that always left Joe stunned—in a good way. She had this regal—something. A calm assurance, a core of serene strength. He knew her history, but he'd never seen anything that even hinted of the wounded bird about her. There was sadness in her, but nothing of the victim.

The truth was, Joe had a terrible crush on Lady Antonia. It was something Sid teased him about. But it wasn't a romantic thing, vampire and werewolf biology just didn't work that way. He admired her greatly—and now she had him all flustered.

"You shouldn't be here," he told her.

"I don't see why not. My daughter needs me. And you are absolutely correct about not wanting to call in the Clan Primes to help with the rescue." She folded her hands in her lap. "If Sidonie needs rescuing, we have adequate troops for the mission right here. I'm a vampire," she reminded him with a brief but impressive show of fangs and claws. "I might not have our kind's full mental strength, but I can make up for it in brute force if I have to. And if it is Justinian that has my little girl, there is no way I can be stopped from going after him."

Joe considered arguing, but he was a werewolf, not a vampire. From his kind's point of view, a mother's protecting her cub was not only a right, it was sacred duty.

"The pack protects the pack," he said.

"Just so." She went very still for a moment, then she asked, "Did you mention Laurent?"

She sounded so calm, so matter-of-fact, but Joe saw the flicker of hunger in her eyes.

"I—" Joe scrubbed his hands across his face. "He . . . He is in town," was all Joe could manage to say.

"We don't think he's involved with Justinian," Daniel spoke up. "Not directly. He doesn't have anything to do with Sid's disappearance."

"Really?" Whatever her true feelings, her

tone was merely curious. "I wonder. It could well be that Justinian and Sidonie have each woven their own schemes around gaining possession of Laurent." She gave a faint, steely smile. "That would make for an interesting clash of wills. Fortunately, Sid's smarter than Justinian. Hopefully, Laurent is as well. Never mind the underlying cause of this crisis." She turned her attention fully on Joe. "You were in the military. What's our plan of attack?"

Joe had remembered something while she'd been speaking. "Laurent's been hanging out with a hunter that's taken on the drug problem."

"Really? Well that bodes well for him, don't you think?"

Joe was skeptical, but he didn't comment. "The hunter has some specialized equipment called a zapper that we're going to acquire," he went on. "I think it gives vampires very bad headaches. Because of your damaged telepathy it probably won't hurt you," he told Antonia. "That'll be one advantage. Another is the drug some of the Tribe boys are using. I was able to take down one that was using. So it'll level the playing field a bit for me and Cathy when we take them on."

"Cathy?" Daniel jumped to his feet. "Cathy's—indisposed."

"She's locked in total full-moon freakout," Joe clarified. "Which means she *needs* to kill things. If we aim her at the right things, it will be good for her. Take my word as a werewolf on this. Besides, Sid's her bud. She'd be really pissed off if she morphed back a couple of days from now and found out we left her out of the fun. And you," he pointed at Daniel. "You have your choice of a gun or a crossbow."

Daniel sighed. "I'll take the gun."

"Good." Joe rubbed his hands together. "Lady Antonia, please tell us you remember how to find this house."

"Of course I do," she answered. "Even though there was a time when my well-meaning matri tried to make me forget."

"I don't think you're lazy," Eden said.

Laurent was awake, but he'd been pretending otherwise. He and Eden were cuddled together spoon fashion, and he'd been relishing the simple comfort of being with her. They'd both slept, but he'd roused and taken bittersweet pleasure in being with her for a peaceful interlude before the next storm broke. He'd absorbed her warmth, tried to ease her bad dreams, adored the way they fit perfectly together even when they weren't engaged in sex.

Though he'd certainly thought about sex. He'd seriously wanted to wake her up by arousing her, and go on from there. But she'd been through a lot, physically and emotionally. She needed the rest.

He'd known the instant she woke, but her words were unexpected.

"If I wasn't lazy I'd have spent the afternoon arranging your escape. If I wasn't lazy I'd have already had my way with you instead of lying here thinking about it. If I wasn't lazy—"

"You said you're too lazy to be a bad guy. I don't think that's it at all. I think you use being lazy as an excuse to keep from being a bad guy. You pretend to yourself that it's too much trouble to bother working up an evil act."

He kissed the back of her neck. "You give me too much credit."

And it was rather sweet that she did.

"You're touched at my vote of confidence," she said.

"You are not psychic," he reminded her.

"Superpowers are not necessary to read people. Body language can be telling."

He stroked a hand down her waist, caressed the curve of her hip and the length of her thigh. "What can you tell from my body language?"

"You're horny. But before that you gave a

contented sigh, and relaxed even more than I thought possible. You're heavy, you know. And I'm still mad at you," she added.

"I don't think I need superpowers to figure that out. And you are still angry with yourself," he countered. "Don't be. You see I told you a lot of things that were true, but out of context."

She squirmed and wriggled in his embrace, and for a few seconds he thought she was trying to arouse him, because that's exactly what her movements did. Then he realized she was trying to turn to face him and he loosened his hold enough to let her. Then he pulled her close again, relishing the feel of her breasts against his chest, and the way his erection pressed up between their bodies.

"Nice," he murmured.

"Animal," she answered, but her tone was more teasing than hostile.

"Your nipples are very hard," he approved.

"You have a hot body. You get me hot. That doesn't signify anything other than—"

"I love you," he said. "Just let me love you."

"You—"

He kissed her to keep her quiet. And to prove that there was something more significant than mutual arousal between them. He could taste the anger that lingered in her, but she craved him as much as he did her, and that was a start.

A start for what? What was the matter with him? Was he still nursing hope for some sort of normal life? They'd had an interlude of a few peaceful hours while the day bled away, that was the most he could hope for.

He drew away from her before his body suppressed all brain function in the need for release. He didn't have the luxury of losing himself right now. Because, if he gave in to indulgence, he was certain Justinian would find a way to use it against him.

"I cannot love right now," he said as he sat up. And that he used the word *love* was dangerous—and frightening.

Eden sat up and put a hand on his shoulder. "I should get out of here. How long until sunset? How many Primes use Dawn?"

"You assume I'm going to help you escape?"

"You did mention something about it earlier."

"So I did. Perhaps I was taunting you."

"You're too lazy to be a villain, remember? And of course I'm not leaving without you, so we'll have to wait until dark. Does Sid use the daylight drugs?"

"So, you're planning my escape as well."

She patted him on the shoulder. "My plan is

to rescue you. There are a lot of connotations to that."

Yes, there were. But before they could discuss any of them, there was a knock on the door.

Their interlude was up. It was time to face Justinian.

Chapter Twenty-four

Eden was shoved into a new room so hard that she ended up on her hands and knees at the foot of a wide bed. The treatment was infuriating, but she stayed where she was until she heard the door close with a firm bang. After she was sure the Prime who'd pushed her was gone, she rose to her feet. That was when she saw the blond woman seated on the bed. She watched Eden with a cool, familiar expression.

"You're Sid Wolf."

"And you are Eden Faveau. We've actually spoken on the phone. It was a bad connection, if you recall."

Sid's voice was rich and deep, and also familiar, though with a more feminine timbre than Laurent's. Her eyes were the same color as her brother's as well.

"It's . . ." Eden looked around the room

where they were both being held prisoner. "Interesting to meet you at last."

"I take it you've been sent to keep me company while the boys enjoy blood and cigars and masculine camaraderie."

Eden nodded. "That's about right."

Sid patted the space next to her on the bed, though she had to use both hands to do it, because she was wearing thick silver cuffs connected by a short chain. Eden didn't know why she was shocked to see that the other woman was restrained. After all, they were women in Tribe territory. She was certain the cuffs were silver.

"Do those hurt?"

"A little."

"Let me see what I can do." Eden sat down. "I see you've been working on them," she said when Sid placed her wrists in Eden's lap. Silver was soft, and one of the links holding the cuffs together was strained and slightly twisted.

"I've had some time on my hands."

"How long have you been a prisoner?"

"Since a few minutes before I was supposed to meet you Friday night. I take it my brother showed up in my place and did exactly the opportunistic things I'd figured he'd do?" When Eden gave the vampire woman a shocked look,

Sid smiled and went on. "I can be a very subtle telepath when I try. But I underestimated the number of Primes Justinian had in town when I let both my and Laurent's whereabouts be known. The original plan was that he'd show up while I was fighting the bad guys, and lend a hand. He would then discover his long-lost sister. Tearful reunion would follow. He'd prove he was worthy of Clan Primehood by helping us wipe out the Dawn dealers. When it didn't work out exactly as I'd hoped, I then considered that maybe he'd meet you anyway, and right and justice would come of it. Has it?" she ended.

Eden almost laughed. She tried to feel used and outraged, but since she wasn't the one who'd been Justinian's prisoner for days, she couldn't work up too much ire at Sid Wolf.

"He's a handful," she admitted. "A mess."

"But I think I see glimpses of potential," Sid said. "Don't you think so?"

Eden couldn't bring herself to comment on this. Her feelings for Laurent were still too confused to talk about with someone else. Especially his sister.

She continued tugging and twisting the silver links, but did steal a glance at the Wolf female. Sid was beautiful, of course, as all vampires were. And Eden was almost ashamed of the flash of jealousy that momentarily went through her.

"Laurent absolutely doesn't want me that way," Sid read her thoughts. "But Justinian assumed that he would."

"Why?" Eden thought about her own question for a moment, and answered it. "Because you look like your mother."

"And Justinian still has it bad for Mom."

"That is *so* sick."

"Yes, from a moral point of view. And no, from a biological and psychic one. His attachment to Antonia is the closest thing Tribe Primes allow themselves to bonding, though what he did to her burned her out."

"So I was right about that. Laurent was wondering," Eden added to Sid's questioning look.

"Really? He thinks about Antonia? Another point in his favor."

"Laurent told me that he thought your mother was dead."

"Justinian got rid of her when he realized he was getting too close to feeling something for her. My guess is that Justinian transferred the love/hate attachment to Laurent. And Laurent's got his own attraction/repulsion thing going with Justinian."

"And you know this, how?"

"Come on, hunter, you know we vampires need each other, need to belong to a kin group. Justinian's pack is the only kin group Laurent's ever known. He wants to escape them, but didn't think he had anywhere else to go. And I know this because about two months ago I finally tracked him down. I wasn't going to tell Mom about him unless he proved worthy. I've been spending some time in Los Angeles and not even telling Joe why. Have you met Joe?"

Eden nodded. "He's been looking for you." But it wasn't the werewolf Eden was interested in. "You found Laurent?"

"Yes. But Justinian found him first. He'd been living away from the pack for years, but Justinian lured him into a revenge scheme against a renegade hunter that had stolen a fortune from the Manticores a long time ago."

"Would this be the Patron person Laurent told me about?"

Sid nodded. "It turned out that the Clans were looking for the Patron as well. I thought it was a good sign that Laurent spent some time with the Shagals and Reynards."

"He said they were boring." Eden chuckled. "It's amazing how cleverly he *didn't* lie to me. I know about the laptop. Did he steal it from the Patron?"

"No, actually. I hate to say it, but the Manticore have every right to the information on that computer. Of course, Laurent wants it for himself rather than letting Justinian have it."

"He traded the computer for you."

Sid smiled happily, and she looked impressed. "I hid in the background and tried to influence him to come to San Diego when he took the computer. Of course, Justinian came, too. I had a plan. Which was totally screwed when the whole tribe showed up to take advantage of this new drug. They've gathered around Justinian because they need the Patron's money to feed their Dawn habit."

"And my people came into it when all the Tribe people started showing up in our town," Eden added.

Sid looked hopefully at Eden. "Will your people be showing up to rescue you anytime soon?"

Eden drew herself out of her awe at the Wolf woman's machinations to sigh. "Doubtful. I quit the corps just before getting captured. They won't think I'm missing, they'll think I'm just gone."

"Pity. We'll cope on our own." Her gaze shifted to the door. "Someone's coming."

Eden stopped working on trying to free Sid and scooted to the end of the bed. Within moments the door opened and a couple of Primes came in to hustle them out of the bedroom.

"A change of scenery at last," Laurent heard Sid whisper under her breath as the females were brought into the room and led his way through the parting crowd.

It was a large, bare room with beamed ceilings, tall, heavily curtained windows, a tiled floor, and a large stone fireplace along one wall. There were a few chairs scattered about, but Justinian was the only one seated, on a throne-like affair in front of the cold fireplace.

Laurent remembered art hanging on the walls in here when he was young, and heavy dark furniture like in the great hall of a castle. The old velvet curtains were faded and shabby. He'd played in here when he could, because the place reminded him of what the Clan citadels in Antonia's stories must be like.

Maybe he shouldn't have listened to Antonia so much. Because here he was, still a romantic at heart, and romantics got into trouble. He held in a sigh as he looked at Eden and Sid, regretting that they were in trouble as well. Eden seemed especially vulnerable, a mortal trapped among monsters. The urge to protect her burned in him.

What the hell was he going to do to get them all out of it?

The room was packed with Primes, many of them eyeing him with less than friendly intentions. He'd noticed at dinner that some of them were on the nervous side. He was used to hostile looks from pack members; testing the limits of other males was how place was determined. But the atmosphere generally wasn't so explosive. It bothered him that normally strict disciplinarian Justinian didn't seem to notice, or was ignoring the tension.

He hated the hungry looks turned on the two women as they were brought forward, but he pretended they weren't important and faced Justinian.

"Quite a crowd," he said. "It looks like a Manticore reunion. Except I notice that old Anastasius isn't here."

"Anastasius is dead."

"Did you kill him?"

"That is how one becomes king of the whole

tribe," the smiling Justinian answered. "I killed him two years ago."

"You didn't mention this when you lured me back to the pack in Los Angeles."

"You didn't need to know it then."

"When Belisarius was still alive, you mean?"

"Yes. Now you need to know that I am king of all the packs. And you, son, are my heir."

"Congratulations—Dad."

Even trying the word on for size Laurent found he didn't like it. *Heir, my ass,* Laurent thought. It was clear from being among this crowd that Justinian wanted someone completely beholden to him to act as an enforcer.

In Laurent's opinion this proved that Justinian was one desperate vampire king.

When Justinian stood, Laurent turned back to face the room. By this time the women were in front of them. The guards made a show of pushing Eden and Sidonie to their knees. Laurent found this whole S&M D/S melodrama embarrassing, but he didn't let his feelings show. He managed a faint, almost indifferent sneer for the benefit of the avidly watching audience.

Justinian put a hand on Laurent's shoulder. Laurent disliked the touch on several levels, especially on the psychic one. Justinian made no secret of the attempt to probe past Laurent's mental shielding.

Oh, please, Laurent thought. And received the sensation of a mental shrug in reply. The games never stopped. Somehow, Laurent had to make them stop.

He couldn't help but look at Eden. But she was being smart and keeping her head down. As was Sid. *They* were aware that it was up to him to make the play that would get them out of here. At least, he hoped that was why they were behaving so passively, rather than having been drugged or hurt.

"I present to you my son, and my second, my beta Prime," Justinian told the gathering. "Laurent of the Manticore."

Loud rumblings came from the crowd in response. Laurent hadn't expected a spontaneous round of applause, but the hostility was much more than usual for this sort of announcement. He remembered the night Justinian had made this same announcement about Belisarius. There had been some applause that night, but Belisarius had been the main bully of the pack for years. That gave him a certain amount of respect and popularity among his peers.

Even so, a fight had broken out, and someone had died.

Laurent surreptitiously flexed his fingers, testing his claws; knowing it was only a matter of time.

"These females are my gift to my heir," Justinian told the gathering, with an expansive gesture toward Eden and Sid.

That should do it, Laurent thought.

Sure enough, a big Prime with a fresh tan stepped forward to get into Laurent's face. "I'll take the human bitch."

"Go ahead," Laurent answered. He waited for Eden's gaze to flash angrily up to meet his, then he smiled at her. He gestured casually toward the other Prime. "If he wants to commit suicide, who am I to stop him, sweetheart?"

Eden laughed.

Sid said sternly, "Laurent."

"I love you, Laurent Wolf," Eden added.

The challenging Prime stepped toward Eden, hand raised to strike her.

"I can't have that," Laurent said, grabbing the Manticore by the wrist.

She loves me.

The glow of pleasure burning in him was ridiculous. It added an extra fillip to the joy of sinking his claws deep into the other vampire's tough hide. Laurent used the hold to swing the Prime away across the room, taking the fight away from the women.

Space quickly cleared in the center of the room. After that things got ugly. Laurent concentrated on what had to be done. All right, he took a certain amount of pleasure in mauling the bastard who'd tried to claim Eden. He *was* Prime.

When it was over, and Laurent was standing over the body of his dead opponent something nagged at him about the fight. The other Prime had been a Dawn user, Laurent could tell by his sun-kissed California tan. His reflexes had also been a bit slower than normal. There'd been a wild look in his eyes that couldn't be accounted for simply by his being a Tribe vampire. It hadn't been an easy victory. But it should have been harder.

We can use this, his sister's words floated as the merest of faint whisper of thought into his head.

Maybe, he thought. But he turned around to find trouble still getting in the way of any escape attempt. Hell, even if the Dawn users were a little on the wussy side, the Manticores still had his team outnumbered three to one.

Right now Justinian was holding Eden, his fist twisted in her hair, her head pulled back exposing her throat. He had a look of sheer maddened fury on his face.

"She called you Wolf," he said to Laurent. "The bitch dared call you—!"

"Let her go," Laurent said, taking a careful step forward. He'd never been so afraid of Justinian before, not in a long lifetime of being afraid of his sire. "Let her go."

Justinian raised his other hand, long, fierce claws extended. He touched them to Eden's cheek. "Not before I mark her."

"She's mine. You have no right."

"All of Manticore is mine. I am king Prime."

A drop of blood oozed from Eden's cheek as Justinian pressed one claw into tender human flesh.

Laurent's first impulse was to rush forward. Everything in him called out to get Eden away from the monster. But that wasn't the way. There was only one certain way to save Eden, to save them all.

And he acknowledged that his whole life had been leading up to this moment.

"You won't be king Prime for long, old man. I challenge."

Laurent turned slowly, though he hated turning his back on Eden's predicament for even a moment. It had to be done right. He had to make it official.

"I challenge!" he shouted, making sure everyone heard, that all the other Primes knew his intentions.

The other Primes sent up a cheer thick with bloodlust.

"I challenge Justinian for leadership of Tribe Manticore!"

Chapter Twenty-five

"The guys on guard are squirrely," Joe said as he returned from his reconnaissance mission. He'd left the rest of his team waiting in the company van a block away from the Manticore stronghold while he carried out the initial part of the plan.

"Good for us," Daniel said.

"I don't understand," Antonia said over Cathy's snarling. She had a firm grip on Cathy's leash.

Right now the office manager was in the form of a hundred-and-ten-pound white and gold wolf. She was a small woman, but her mass made her a formidable creature when morphed into werewolf form. Someday Cathy would learn how to control the change, and manage to keep sentient as well while in morphed form. Being a werewolf would be fun. But for now the full moon took away everything but the darker, dangerous cravings of werewolf nature. The need to hunt and kill was about to come in handy.

"There are two vampires patrolling the grounds, but they're not really paying attention," Joe explained. "I overheard part of a very intense *Pulp Fiction*-esque conversation about sunrises."

"That you managed to get close enough to overhear them bodes well," Antonia said. "They must be Dawn users."

"Which means we can take them," Daniel said.

He was holding a Glock modified to fire silver-tipped bullets Sid had recently developed. She'd said that it might prove useful in a missing-persons case.

"I wish we'd found some more useful equipment when we broke in to the vampire hunter's place," Daniel added.

"It would have been nice if the vampire hunter had been there," Joe said. "We could have used her help. At least we got the zapper."

"Where is it?" Daniel asked.

Joe had carried it in a backpack when he approached Justinian's house. "I was listening to the sunrise conversation while I set the zapper up to save us some time. It's hidden by a bush at the back of the house, near the tall windows you remembered, Lady Antonia. You're right about that being the best insertion point."

He'd also left some clothes for later. Now he started to quickly undress.

"I'm glad to be of help. Now what?" Antonia asked.

"Now we move out," Joe said. "Take out the guards, turn on the zapper—your job, Daniel, I can't do it with my nose. Then we break in and save Sidonie."

Joe took a deep breath, and morphed into his black wolf form.

"Hurray for us," Daniel said.

"Let's go," Antonia said, and set off at a vampire's swift pace, the blond werewolf loping at her side.

"Well, well," Justinian said. "I was hoping for this."

"I bet you were, old man," Laurent said. "Did you foresee beating me?"

"Of course."

Justinian tossed Eden aside. She landed squarely on top of Sid, and the women went down in a heap. Laurent stepped around them, concentrating on his sire.

"I foresaw you needing to be put in your place one last time, *boy*. You'll be my heir, but I'll tame you once and for all first."

"Yeah, yeah, yeah," Laurent complained. "Heard it before."

Laurent waited and watched the older Prime. He was in no hurry. Once upon a time—many times—he had blindly, mindlessly attacked. And every time led to the same painful, humiliating ending.

Now he had the patience of an adult. And something besides himself to fight for: Eden. Sid. Freedom.

"Come and get me, old man," he invited.

As Eden fell hard on top of Sid, the vampire whispered, "Help me!" and shoved her manacled hands toward Eden's face. "One more tug."

There was a wild look in the vampire's eyes that shocked Eden, then she grinned. Sid was on the side of the angels. She sure hoped Laurent was on the side of the angels, because she'd never heard anyone sound so dangerous before.

A deep, animal snarl from Justinian made her flinch. She felt the rush of air as the older Prime leapt toward Laurent, and her adrenaline spiked with fear.

Laurent needed her!

Eden would have rushed into the fight, but Sid grabbed her. "Help me! Then we can both help Laurent!"

This got through to Eden. A fight to the death raged only a few feet away. She had to make sure the one who died wasn't Laurent.

None of the Primes were paying any attention to a pair of lowly females. Eden wrapped her hands around Sidonie's wrists and joined the vampire in breaking the chain.

Sid was right, it took only a few moments.

But the instant Sid was free and on her feet she covered her ears with her hands and slammed back down to her knees.

And she wasn't the only one.

Eden looked around as vampires began to howl, run around like maniacs, and attack each other. She whirled around desperately, looking for Laurent. She spotted him and Justinian in front of the fireplace, struggling back and forth across the floor. They were both covered in blood. Justinian's face was a mask of pain. She saw that Laurent recognized what was going on, and was working through the disorientation.

"That's my boy," she murmured, and quickly turned back to Sid. She grabbed Sid by the shoulders. "Look at me!"

It took a moment, but Sid's gaze finally focused on Eden. "Hurts."

"Ignore it. Fight it. Get up. You're tougher than these Manticore bastards."

"Damn right," Sid answered, on a hiss of pain.

Eden stepped back, letting Sid get to her feet on her own. She watched as Sidonie Wolf transformed from a beautiful woman into a beautiful woman with long fangs and sharp, vicious claws.

"I forgot that females can do that too."

Sid forced a laugh. "So do Tribe males," she said. Then she bared her fangs and jumped on the back of the nearest Prime.

Eden didn't have any of the usual weapons of her vampire slaying trade, but she didn't let a little thing like that stop her. What was the use of sweating through years of martial arts training if she couldn't beat up on some scum vampires that were being zapped?

The world wanted to go red, but this was no time to let it. Discipline and stubbornness were the best weapons Laurent had right now. He actually preferred the pain from the zapper to what he'd been going through moments before.

You're a fool, boy. Weak. Mine.

Justinian bombarded him with such thoughts from the instant the fight started.

You can't hurt me. You know who your master is.

The words were deadlier than the blows.

Laurent was physically stronger, faster.

But Justinian was better at twisting the knife.

Until the zapping began, Laurent had spent too much energy defending against the insidious thoughts that slid past his shielding and tried to wreck his heart and soul.

Eden loved him. He had a sister. Antonia was safe.

This armor covered old wounds, kept him in the fight, but it was new to him.

You're losing more blood than I am, Laurent pointed out, and spun around to rake claws across Justinian's back.

The older Prime howled. And as he did the windows exploded inward. In this moment Laurent noticed that the room was full of violence—Primes battling with Primes. Sid and Eden were in the thick of it, fighting back to back.

"Good girls."

Then a pair of werewolves came through the broken windows, followed by more humanoid shapes. A gun fired. A Prime screamed and fell. Help had arrived.

Laurent was laughing when he grappled once more with Justinian. This time he went in for the kill.

Joe blessed whoever had come up with Dawn, because there sure were a lot of vampires in the room. But fortunately, the drug users were weaker than the rest, and most of the vampires were users. This gave him and Cathy more than half a chance. The zapper had set all the Primes off already, the pain spreading the always volatile into a riot. Cathy was already spreading bloody carnage. Joe took a quick look around to see how the rest of his team was doing. Sid was in the fray, so was Antonia. Much to his surprise he saw the human hunter smashing a heavy chair over a vampire's head. And, my, my, there was brother Laurent. Satisfied, he let out a warrior's howl and leapt into the riot.

"Give me that!"

"What?" the blond guy in glasses asked. He was standing with his back to the fireplace, holding the weapon up, taking very careful aim, but hesitating with his shots.

"That's not the way to do it. Give me the gun."

He pointed the gun at her. "Who are you?"

"Something you're not—a pro. Give me."

"Duck."

She did. He fired. The vampire that had been coming up behind her let out a very satisfying scream. Silver bullets, she supposed, or garlic embedded in the shells.

"Good work," she acknowledged, and snatched the weapon from his hands. In turn she tossed him the chair leg she'd been using as a club.

"Hey!" he called, but she was already moving away. The gun was warm, heavy, and reassuring in her hands. She had plans for this mother.

"You can't kill me."

"Wanna bet?" Laurent answered.

Justinian was panting hard, bruised and bloody, reeling from exhaustion and suffering the effects of the zapper. But he wouldn't stop. And Laurent was frightened that the old Prime might be right. As hard as he tried, as many chances as he got, he kept pulling the killing blow.

The worst part was that Laurent was certain it had nothing to do with the way Justinian had conditioned him. But pity nagged at him. It didn't feel like weakness, but it was stupid.

He took another swing at Justinian, this time

raking bloody gouges across his throat. Justinian's head was thrown back. This gave Laurent a quick view past Justinian's shoulder. He saw Eden running toward him, with a gun in her hand. She was intent on him, not aware of the Prime rushing up on her.

"Behind you!" Laurent shouted.

But she reacted an instant too slowly. The Prime tackled her. The gun flew from her hand. Laurent instantly forgot Justinian. He rushed to help Eden. Laurent scooped up the gun and fired without hesitation.

Eden gave Laurent a grateful look. She was grinning, and her eyes were shining. Such fierceness was a good thing in a vampire's mate.

She started to say something as she pushed out from under the dead vampire.

"Antonia!"

Justinian's tortured shout drowned out everything else in the world. He looked up, just as Justinian rushed past him.

Then Laurent caught sight of the woman in the center of the room, and his jaw dropped. She was as beautiful as silver in the moonlight. So beautiful it was painful to look at her. A vision. A memory.

"Antonia?" He could barely speak for the joyous pain.

"Laurent!" Eden shouted in his ear. She shook his shoulder. "Do something!"

In an instant Laurent came to the real world. He raised the gun and fired. Three rounds. One in the head. Two in the back. He hoped to hell he hit the bastard's heart. At any rate, he felt Justinian die. It was as if a dark weight lifted off the universe.

He had no idea if the shout of joy that went up was from Eden, Sid, or himself. The chaos around them was quieting down, but he didn't care. The zapper stopped shrieking into his brain, and he hardly noticed. Laurent's interest in that moment was only on Antonia.

He had to step across Justinian's lifeless body to reach her. It was only when they were close that he noticed that her lips were drawn back, and her fangs were out. There was a part of him that had forgotten she was a vampire.

"You're beautiful."

"You've grown," was her reply as she looked up to meet his gaze.

"So, Sid, how you doing?" Joe said, coming up to his partner.

He was back in human form after jumping outside to turn off the zapper. He'd paused long enough to pull on his stashed clothing and a pair of sandals. The room was strewn with the bodies of the vampires who hadn't run away. The good guys were the only ones left standing.

"You don't look any worse for wear," he added. "You do know we had to take time off from some important cases to find you." He gave a one-shoulder shrug. "Of course, if a missing-person's agency can't find one of its own people . . . "

"I detect a certain amount of annoyance in your tone," she answered. "Do you want me to look worse for wear?"

"No." He grabbed her and hugged her. "I was terrified for you."

"Aw," she said, and grazed her fangs gently across his shoulder before she stepped back. A sign of affection from a vampire to a werewolf. "Thanks for the rescue. I knew you'd figure it out."

Cathy was sitting on her haunches at Sid's side. Sid's telepathy was the only thing that could calm the bitten werewolf during the full-moon seizures. Now that the fighting was over, Cathy certainly needed to be controlled.

Joe glanced over his shoulder at the reunion taking place in the center of the room. So far Lady Antonia and Laurent were just looking at each other. "What's he doing here?" Joe asked, not trying to conceal his hostility.

"Same thing you are. Rescuing the fair maidens."

She stepped closer to Antonia and Laurent, and Joe followed, confused. Daniel came up to put his arm around Sid's shoulder. The vampire hunter joined them but without sparing a glance for anyone but Laurent.

Eden didn't know why, but she was more frightened for Laurent at this moment than she had been when he was fighting Justinian.

Don't reject him, she thought at Antonia. *Don't you dare.*

"I . . ." Where to start? What to say? "I looked for you," Laurent finally told Antonia. "I called but—"

"I couldn't have answered." She glanced disdainfully at Justinian's corpse. "He saw to that." She put a hand on his arm. "It was years before I could look for you." This time she looked toward Sid. "We looked for you."

"Sidonie told me."

"We have a lot to talk about, Laurent."

"Let's get out of here, first."

She nodded. Then her expression turned

stern. The look in Antonia's eyes was pure steel as she looked him over from head to toe, then looked him in the eye. "Choose."

Her tone was pure steel as well. The voice of Lady Antonia, head of House Antonia of Clan Wolf. Laurent wasn't confused for a moment about what she meant.

Choose.

It occurred to him that he was now technically the king Prime of Tribe Manticore. Ironic as that was, he could imagine the wicked possibilities.

Then he thought about Eden and glanced sideways at her. She looked so bloody, intensely hopeful.

I love you, Laurent Wolf!

"Wolf," he answered his mother, knowing full well every difficult thing the choice entailed. "I choose Clan Wolf."

"A wise decision," Antonia said. She smiled. "I think your young woman makes you better than you want to be."

He turned to Eden, and she rushed into his embrace. Never mind everything else that had happened, was happening; he couldn't do anything but kiss her. The warmth of her, the eagerness of her response; this was the reassurance that they were alive. Everything was going to be all right.

It made him smile against Eden's lips when Sid's gang started to applaud.

When they broke the kiss, he kept his arm around Eden's waist. He turned them to face Antonia. "This is my—"

"Fiancé," Eden piped up.

"Fiancé," he agreed, on a rush of pleasure. Fiancé. Yeah. "Future bondmate is the term," he told Eden.

"Well, then," Antonia said, holding out her arms at last. "Welcome home, both of you."

Epilogue

Seven months later

"I don't know about this new look of yours," Eden said, taking a step back from Laurent's embrace. From the hungry, eager way she felt you'd have thought she hadn't seen him in a year. Still, her expression was a bit dubious. "I finally get my trip to Hawaii, and I come home to find that you've cut your hair."

While they'd spent a lot of time apart in the last months, this three weeks had been the longest time without any physical contact since Laurent entered what he thought of as Clan Boy Boot Camp. They'd only been allowed a few phone calls and e-mails.

While she'd been sunning on beaches and finally visiting her volcano, he'd been undergoing treatment at the Clans' clinic up in Los Angeles. Along with drug treatments to allow him to function in the daylight, he'd had a lot of counseling to go through.

And they'd brought in a big dog for that; old Barak of Clan Shagal to give him a lot of long, hard talking-to, and a certain amount of physical thumping as well. Tough love. That was what Elder Barak was all about.

Barak had been inside his head and out, finding the curves and quirks and phantoms that even the Wolfs' best psychic healers hadn't been able to find. Laurent came away from the experience feeling like his brain had not only been washed, it had been waxed and detailed.

"My therapist convinced me that the long hair was a connection with my Tribe past," Laurent told Eden. "Cut the hair, sever the connection. Get it?"

She nodded. "You're going to grow it back, right?"

He grinned. "Oh, yeah."

They couldn't take *all* the bad boy out of him. He didn't think it was likely he was ever going to be a model citizen.

"I like you a little rough around the edges," Eden said, picking up on his intent without having to read his mind.

He liked that she could know him so well without any special psychic talents. Correction, he loved it.

She kissed him again, long and slow and thorough, totally uncaring that they were standing on the crowded sidewalk outside the airport baggage claim area.

"I missed you," she said when she let him up for air. "We both did."

He touched her expanded abdomen and got a head-butt from the inside in response. He grinned. "Toni's as tough as her mama." And unlike her mama, their daughter was already showing signs of being psychic from inside the womb. They were going to call her Antonia Sidonie Wolf.

It was a good thing they were already an official couple by the time Eden discovered she was pregnant. If not, he'd probably have had the Clan and the hunters after him for that indiscretion. Eden had been right to worry about their not using birth control the first time they'd made love. She'd pointed out then that it only took once.

So now, here they were, going to be parents.

He took her hand, and they went to the car that was waiting for them. Sid was waiting behind the wheel, totally oblivious to the traffic cop trying to wave her to move on. Once they were settled in the back seat, she turned the car out into the heavy traffic.

"Are you ready for this?" she asked him, once she'd greeted Eden.

"You'll like it," Eden assured him, patting his hand. "I know I do. Was I missed?"

"Terribly. Even Cathy likes having Eden around," Sid assured him.

After the scattering of the Manticores, Eden had rejoined the hunters to finish cleaning out the Dawn dealers, and he and Sid had helped with the op. For him it was a way of proving his intent to turn over a new leaf—and it hadn't hurt his emotional well-being to be there to watch Eden's back.

Then she'd finally quit the vampire hunting business. Her family had been upset with her on several counts, but at least her father and brothers were still talking to her. They'd even grudgingly showed up at the wedding.

She'd also left her job to take a position with a company that operated within her new world. Bleythin Investigations had acquired a new investigator who specialized in computer security.

Another thing he'd done to prove his Clanworthiness was give up any right to whatever was in the Patron's computer. It was Manticore property—and he was Wolf. So much for the treasure that could have been his if he'd gotten Eden to break into the data *before* his miraculous reformation.

Now he was about to take on one more Clan Prime responsibility.

He glanced at the fresh wolf's-head tattoo on the inside of his right wrist. He hadn't been required to take the vow to protect and serve, but he'd decided to give it a shot. It had made his mother proud. And Sid. And Eden most of all.

Serving humanity had to start somewhere, so at Joe's prompting, Laurent had also taken a position with Bleythin Investigations. He was going to help find missing persons, starting as soon as they got to the office.

He looked at Eden and touched the tip of her long, elegant nose, drawing a smile from her.

"I never thought I'd have a day job," he told her.

Enter the world
of Susan Sizemore. . . .

And read a sneak preview from

Primal Heat

Available July 2006
from Pocket Star Books

Primal Heat

"Your in-laws are scary," Phillipa Eliot told her sister, who was a lovely and not-in-the-least blushing bride.

Phillipa leaned against the terrace railing next to her sister, and took another sip of very good champagne. The hot wind that blew in off the desert didn't bother her. Heck, she was from Phoenix; there was no way Las Vegas could get hotter than home. The dry air did make her thirsty, though; she thought she was on her fifth glass of champagne.

Josephine's eyes went wide. "What do you mean by scary?"

Phillipa looked at the people dancing at the wedding reception in the hotel ballroom. "They make me feel like I've crashed the supermodels' annual ball."

Jo laughed. "Yeah, I know exactly what you mean." Her gaze didn't leave her new husband, who was currently dancing with their mother. "Isn't he—?"

"Large," Phillipa cut in.

"I was going to say cute."

Phillipa laughed. "Of course you were."

She thought that the hulking groom was probably the least handsome man there. Not that the muscular Marcus Cage didn't have enough charm and charisma for three normal males. It seemed to run in the Cage family, and among all their friends. The women were amazingly beautiful, mostly in a dark and mysterious way. And the men—good lord!

They'd been hitting on her since the rehearsal dinner the night before. It had been quite a stimulating experience.

Phillipa took a moment to fan her face. She wasn't sure if it was the champagne, or the mere thought of the men at the reception that was causing the warmth that stirred through her. There was something special about this bunch; after all, she was a cop and used to working around hunky, hard-bodied, macho men. Not only was she used to it, she liked it. But the Cages and their friends had so much going for them in the confident, sexy male department that they were downright daunting.

"It's not that I don't like the Cage clan," Phillipa explained.

"Family," Josephine said. "They're a family, not a clan."

"What difference does that make?"

Jo laughed. "Never mind, and I can't explain anyway. If I did, they'd probably have to kill you. It's a joke between Marc and me," she added quickly.

Phillipa let it go. Far be it from her to try to interpret the private language of newlywed lovebirds, especially after five glasses of champagne.

She looked at her empty glass, and said, "I'm switching to water." One of the groom's hunky relatives was heading their way, and his gaze was fixed on her. "Right now," she added, and left so he'd have to ask her sister to dance instead of her.

The band stopped playing as she skirted the dance floor and she noticed Marc heading for Jo, and Mom heading toward where Dad waited for her. Phillipa smiled, appreciating the devotion of the happy couples. At the same time, she had to fight off a twinge of sadness at being alone herself. She blamed the self-pity on the champagne, because she had no one to blame for breaking up with Patrick but Patrick. You'd think with all the gorgeous men in the place, she'd be more interested in hooking up with one of them.

Maybe I don't want another macho man. Maybe that was why all the groom's male relatives set off alarm bells she couldn't explain.

The band started playing again as she reached the bar.

"Not more Queen," a man said behind her.

The disgust in his voice amused her, and the deep British accent was intriguing. As the band continued with "Another One Bites the Dust," she took the water the bartender handed her, then turned around. She hadn't noticed the man standing behind her before, though she was somehow aware of his presence before he spoke. His hair was wavy and sandy brown, his eyes green and surrounded by laugh lines. He had a lived-in face; a dangerous face.

"I know what you mean," she told him. "If they play 'Fat-Bottomed Girls,' I'm out of here."

"I'll join you," he answered.

"And if they start playing a lot of Def Leppard, Jo will run away screaming."

Phillipa moved away from the crowd surrounding the bar. The newcomer followed after her as she edged around the dance floor on her way back to the terrace.

"Who's Jo, and what's wrong with Def Leppard? I'm a proud son of Sheffield myself," he added.

"Where's that?"

"Northern England. Same hometown as the Lep—?"

"And what do you mean, who's Jo?" Phillipa stopped and confronted him. "You *are* a guest at the Elliot-Cage wedding, aren't you?"

His smile was devastating, showing deep dimples and crinkling the lines around his eyes. "I'm the best man."

Irritation flared over the heat that had been roused by his smile. "You're Matt Bridger!" she accused. "You very nearly ruined this wedding!"

"It's not my fault my plane was late."

"You were supposed to have arrived yesterday."

He gestured at the boisterous people filling the crowded room. "It doesn't look like I was missed."

"One of my brothers stepped in as best man."

"Then it all turned out all right." He crossed his arms over his wide chest, and moved close to her. "I don't know what you have to be angry about."

"I'm angry on my sister's behalf."

"Why's that?"

"She's Jo Elliot."

"The singer in Def Leppard?"

"The bride!"

Even as she indignantly declared this, Phillipa realized that Matt Bridger was perfectly aware of it, and that he was teasing her.

She stepped closer to him. Suddenly they were toe to toe and nose to nose. He put an arm around her waist, drawing her even closer. She was caught by the masculine heat and scent of him. "You're provoking me on purpose."

The back of his hand brushed across her cheek. "Yes."

Her knees went weak and she almost dropped her glass. She didn't notice where it went when he took it out of her hand.

"Dance with me."

"Yes."

And she never wanted to dance with anyone else.

He drew her onto the dance floor, and they started dancing slowly to the fast music. It was the most natural thing in the world to gaze into this stranger's eyes and press her body against his, soft and hard blending. They didn't share a word while the music played, yet the communication between them was deep and profound. She'd known him forever, been waiting for him forever. It was all too perfect to make any sense.

When the music stopped, she would've kept right on dancing, but Matt turned them off the dance floor. Her arms stayed draped around his wide shoulders and her gaze stayed locked with his. His palms pressed against the small of her back, large and warm and possessive.

Despite this intimate closeness, Phillipa tried to regain her sanity.

"We've just met."

"And you're really not that kind of girl."

"What kind of girl?"

"The sort who snuggles up to a stranger the

moment they meet. And I'm not that sort of man." He flashed that devastating smile at her again. "Mostly."

"Then why are we—"

"We have more than snuggling in mind."

"Yes, but—"

"I have a theory."

She didn't want to hear his theory. "Kiss me."

Fingers traced across her lips. "Soon."

His touch left her sizzling. This was crazy! She should be embarrassed. Phillipa took a deep breath and made an effort to step away. She managed to move maybe an inch, a small triumph for public decency.

"Like calls to like," he said, pulling her back to him.

She lost interest in decency. "I'm a cop."

"Fancy that." As the music started again, he took her by the hand. The connection was electric. "Come on."

She held back. This was her last chance to stay virtuous. "I don't—"

"Listen."

She did, and laughed. "Oh my God, 'Fat-Bottomed Girls.'"

"You said you'd leave if they played it."

"Left alone with big fat Fanny—she was such a naughty nanny . . . " sang the band.

"Matt Bridger, let's get out of here."

They headed toward the door, but he stopped after a few steps. "One thing, first."

"What?"

"Your name."

"Phillipa Elliot."

At least she wasn't about to fall into reckless abandon with a *total* stranger, now.

He tilted his head and gave her a quick, thorough once-over. What he saw was a tall blond woman in a strapless tea-length teal satin bridesmaid's dress.

"I know, I don't look like a Phillipa," she said. "But who does?"

"Pardon me for saying so, but that is an unfortunate name for a Yank, isn't it?"

"I'm used to it."

"Good. It suits you."

The band started in on the chorus again, and they ran for the door.

They didn't kiss until they were in the elevator, coming together in a rush of heat. His mouth was hard and demanding on hers, and she responded just as fiercely. The way he caressed her made her feel naked despite the satin dress and layers of undergarments. His fingers tracing along her bare shoulders and the back of her neck drove her wild. She knew this was crazy, but she didn't care.

Until she noticed that her skirt was hiked up around one hip and his hand was stroking the inside of her thigh. It felt wonderful.

"We're not exactly private here," she reminded him. "Hotel"—she gasped as his fingers moved higher—"security."

"Room key," was his answer.

He stopped long enough for her to fumble open her tiny purse, and the doors slid open onto the fourteenth floor just as she pulled out the black plastic key card.

"This is it." She didn't remember pressing the button for her floor, but she hadn't told him where her room was. Odd. At least the room wasn't far from the elevators, and they were there within a few moments.

Inside, he whirled her around onto the bed.

"You make me dizzy," she said as he leaned over her and she looked into his green eyes.

"Only dizzy?"

There was a wicked glint in those eyes, and a world of sensual promise in his slight smile. There was also something dangerous about his deep, slightly rough voice. The sound of it sent a thrill through her.

"Say something else."

He chuckled. "What is it about Yank women and English accents?"

"Don't complain if it helps you get laid," she told him.

He laughed again. "Would this sound seductive in Sheffield?" he asked, doing a very good job of mimicking an American accent.

"Yes. But it's not just your accent that's sexy. You have gorgeous lips," she added. When she traced them with a finger, he nipped it. "And sharp teeth."

"Oh, yes." He kissed her throat.

Her blood raced as warm lips pressed against her tender skin. His hand brushed across the satin covering her breast, sparking the overwhelming desire to have his naked flesh against hers.

A moment later he tugged her to her feet and pulled on the dress's long zipper. As the dress pooled around her feet, his thumb slid slowly down the length of her bare spine. She arched against him.

"Skin on skin, just like you want," he murmured. His lips were close to her ear. Then they were on her throat.

There was a moment of sharp pain, followed by blinding ecstasy. When her mind cleared from the blissful overload, they were back on the bed once more, and he was as naked as she was. She ran her hands across his chest, and appreciating the sight and texture of hard muscles and hot flesh.

"You are so sweet," he told her.

"I'm more than sweet." She pulled his head down and kissed him hard.

"You're also hot," he agreed.

He kissed her gently, on the lips and on the cheek. But she was aware of the edge of ferocity he was holding back. Then his head moved down and his tongue swirled around one hard nipple, and then the other.

She moaned, and inside the needy sound she heard his voice. *I'm trying to stay civilized.*

Don't, she answered.

His touch grew rougher then, and her responses were just as frantic. He kissed and bit her all over. Each pinprick of pain that followed the soft brush of lips brought her a flash of mounting pleasure.

The contrast was maddening. Wonderful.

With each flash, the heat pooling in her belly grew and spread until the orgasms became one long, continuous wave of ecstasy. She didn't think it could get better—until he was inside her, filling her with hard, fast strokes that drowned her in fiery sensation. She clung to him, rose to meet him with the same frantic energy, wanted nothing but more.

More was what he gave her. She gave herself

up to him, blended with him, blood, mind and soul, and he gave himself to her. She was complete with him, whole with him, until one last, shattering explosion sent her over the edge and into darkness.

"That was—" Phillipa sighed, unable to describe the experience. Now she understood why sex was called The Little Death. Maybe only good sex was called that. Great sex.

Little sparks of pleasure were still shooting through her. She was exhilarated and exhausted at the same time. She was completely content to come back to reality to find herself lying across Matt, with her breasts pressed against the hard muscles of his bare chest. She rested her cheek against the warmth of his skin, and breathed in his male scent.

"It certainly was," Matt answered.

He was lying on a pile of pillows, his hands propped behind his head, a smug smile curving his beautiful mouth. She caught the sparkle of green in his half-closed eyes.

"You look like a well-fed cat," she told him.

"Very well-fed," he answered. "But still hungry."

He pulled her up the length of his body for a kiss. His mouth was as insistent and needy as if they hadn't just made love. As his hands began to roam, he made her hungry all over again.

This time she was able to keep her head long enough to say, "Maybe we shouldn't." His mouth circled a nipple. "Oh, God! I mean—there's supposed to be photos—and—wedding stuff." She was too deep into the pleasure to remember just what. "We'll be missed."

He nuzzled her, and his voice was muffled from between her breasts. "Do you really care?"

"Nooo—yes! We'll be missed. I should be there. She's my sis—" She suddenly became very aware of his erection, and her hand closed around it. She had to touch him, to stroke him. "I shouldn't be doing this."

"You better not stop."

His hungry growl sent a needy shiver through her. His voice was enough to make her melt. "But—"

This sort of thing happens at family gatherings all the time.

"What happens?"

People disappear to make love. It's a way to celebrate the bonding.

"That's nice." It occurred to Phillipa that there was something odd about this conversation. "Did you just say something inside my head?"

Not that you'll recall. Relax, sweetness. Make love to me.

"All right." It was all she wanted to do anyway.

A carousel music version of "Ode to Joy" woke Phillipa up, but her first thought was, *I belong with this man.* When she came a little farther awake she realized that the noise was a cell phone ringing, and that she was lying naked in a dark hotel room with Matt Bridger. She couldn't think of anywhere better to be, and snuggled closer to him while Beethoven kept playing.

Eventually Matt grunted and rolled over to pick the phone up from the nightstand. "Mike, if you're drunk, you're a dead lobo." Whatever the answer was, it made Matt sit up. His muscles bunched with tension. "Where and when? Right. I'm not alone."

Phillipa decided to let him ride out this emergency in privacy, and took the opportunity to slide out of bed for the bathroom. She took her time using the facilities and drinking a glass of water.

As she stepped back into the dark bedroom she was aware of its emptiness. The musky tang of sex was still in the air—but even before she turned on a light and saw the rumpled, empty bed, she knew he was gone.